"Where is he?" Rage leaped into her voice. "Tell me where Ben is! I want to know now. Where is my son?"

The man was gaping at her, his eyes round. Her voice rose, increased in volume. She said, "Has my husband sent you here to kidnap him? Where's Ben? Where have you got him? You'd better tell me!" She pounded the table in front of him, her jaws actually snapping with rage. Anger suffused her chest like passion, and she felt it running in her veins. She knew that nothing could stop her from making this man tell her what she wanted to know.

He rose clumsily from his chair, trying to shake off her grip on his arm. "I don't know what you're talking about, lady. I just came here to get some forms straightened out, just doing my job." He resorted to anger himself, in an attempt to quench hers. "What are you, some kind of nut? I didn't even know you had a little boy."

"Then why did you ask me about him? How did you recognize his picture?"

He began to stammer. "What is this, anyhow?" He jerked away from the table, scattering the papers with his heavy hand. He turned to look at the photograph again, reaching for it. Just before his fingers closed around the frame, Mercer crashed the Queen Anne candlestick into the side of his skull.

The man fell slowly, without a sound.

KEEPAWAY

Martha Moffett

BANTAM BOOKS
NEW YORK · TORONTO · LONDON · SYDNEY · AUCKLAND

KEEPAWAY

A Bantam Book / November 1989

ISBN 0-553-28184-4

Published simultaneously in the United States and Canada

*Bantam Books are published by Bantam Books, a division of Bantam
Doubleday Dell Publishing Group, Inc. Its trademark, consisting of the
words ''Bantam Books'' and the portrayal of a rooster, is Registered in
U.S. Patent and Trademark Office and in other countries. Marca Regis-
trada. Bantam Books, 666 Fifth Avenue, New York, New York 10103.*

KEEPAWAY

CHAPTER ONE

When Mercer first arrived in the southern coastal fishing village with its flaming sunsets and hard white streets and shuttered windows, it seemed cold to her. Things had a hard edge. She looked at the clacking palms, the enameled colors of the tropical plants, the sharp blue of the sky. "It's photo-realism," she joked to Benjamin. The real thing did not seem to possess any depth, while the paintings she had seen hanging in smart galleries in the city hinted at something profound in the American landscape.

The truth was, Mercer did not at all like the place she had run to, although its very ugliness, its obscurity, had a protective quality. *Relax, Merce*, she advised herself. The mechanics of recognition involved expectancy. An old friend who would greet her warmly in the galleries of the Metropolitan Museum of Art might very well fail to recognize her in this seedy little town. Mercer and Cormack and their son Benjamin belonged on Fifth Avenue, when they were not at Cormack's family home in Connecticut. Mercer and Ben were to be found every afternoon at the playground in Central Park at Ninety-sixth Street, their natural setting. Mercer and Cormack were to be seen at the ballet, at parties and gallery openings and first nights. Twice a year they could be found relaxing on the beach at Antigua, on the slopes at Aspen. That's where their friends expected to run into them during appropriate seasons. No one would look for Mercer McCormack in Briney Breezes, Florida. Where was it, anyway? Near Palm Beach? On the Gulf Coast? They'll never find us, she thought.

But what about last week, she reminded herself, when you saw that stranger walking around the empty lot? That spooked you, didn't it?

From her upstairs bedroom in the narrow town house on a cypress-hung canal, she had watched a lone man approach through the brush on the opposite side of the canal. Even as she watched him, she told herself that it was silly to think he was spying on her—like Ptolemy thinking the stars wheeled around his own head. Self-deluding too. Soon she'd be thinking every stranger was a menace. She might as well think that her husband had opened an atlas, placed a finger on the map, and said, "There. That's it. That's where she will be," dispatching agents to locate her and Benjamin and bring them back. Not this time. This time she hadn't left a clue. Nevertheless, she closed the upstairs curtains and went to sit downstairs, playing a game with Benjamin on the living room floor and watching the clouds light up with the colors of evening.

In the twilight, the man appeared again, swinging a fish from a hand line. She realized then that beyond the empty field on the other side of the canal lay a freshwater canal running from the lake to the coast. When the spillway was open, the fishing would be irresistible to a man who knew the shortcut through the weed-filled lot. She had jumped up in a whirl of relief, talking to Ben, turning on the lights, running outside to shout across the canal, "Do you want to sell your fish? I'd like to buy it. Do you want to sell it?" She had frightened him, poor man.

No, no one would think of looking for her here, she reassured herself. No one would remember that her mother had died here, in a condominium south of Palm Beach. Mercer had been at school still. They had telephoned her to come down. She had not known until she arrived that the little coastal settlement had a name of its own, that it was not part of Palm Beach, but "in the county," as they said. It was a place she had never expected to visit twice in her lifetime. Yet here she was again.

Anyone who knew her would probably expect her to go to earth in Boston or San Francisco. London, Paris, Stockholm. She could picture herself in some places, not at all in others. Not here, for instance. She couldn't imagine herself here. That was how she had made the choice. It was a place without natives, a place where no one looked at home.

The malleability of the Florida landscape shocked her. One day broad tracts of saw grass and banyan might sway in the breeze; the next day they might be scraped away and replaced with a golf course, willows, and orange-colored ponds reflecting nothing. Just last week, driving back to the house from an interview for a job which she didn't get, because they wanted someone with experience, she had seen a bamboo grove—not young plants, but a grove of mature trees—along the highway. The stand of plants effectively hid a sprawling trailer camp and could be described as an improvement, but she knew the bamboo had not been there the week before. You'd never treat the landscape in Maine that way, she thought. You'd never expect to go out some morning and find things had been shifted around or replaced. "The view shouldn't be so arbitrary," she said to Benjamin.

After she and Benjamin had settled into the house on the canal, she noticed that the fields and the sides of the roads were feathered over with weeds that looked silver or wheat-colored in the sun, and that the house was full of a burnt sugar smell from the fired canefields west of town. Her early impression that there were no seasons was proved wrong as she began to detect changes unrelated to temperature. They first experienced an autumn of sorts. After that there was a period of time when the sun went down as soon as Benjamin came home from school, and the two of them lit the candles in the Queen Anne candlestick and dined in a warm wintry blackness.

In another six weeks, with no change in temperature, the season changed again. The orange trees, still bearing bright fruit from the last harvest, put on a new frosting of white, and the scent of orange blossoms poured through the window and washed over her bed every night. One evening, after dinner, the light lingered in the west over the distant highway that marked the coast from the swampy inland, and a neighbor, a young fisherman, came over to toss a Frisbee for Benjamin to catch in the pale lilac twilight.

"Ma, watch!" Benjamin made the Frisbee rise and bank on the air before it slipped down. "Ma" was something new, part of their new small-town life. At first she refused to answer to it, but finally she had given in. She supposed it might even be a promotion of sorts. It was still "Mommy" at bedtime, and a shrill "Mer-CER!" in times of stress.

Johntie, the deaf young man who was their neighbor, caught the Frisbee and spun it back. He smoothed his T-shirt and tucked it into the narrow band of his cutoff jeans. He had been an athlete at school, he had told her in combination signing and limited speech. He was good at track and field and throwing the discus. Glancing from her kitchen window in the early mornings as she packed a school lunch for Benjamin, Mercer sometimes watched Johntie jogging along the back lane where people parked their cars and trailered boats.

"My turn!" She stepped onto the lawn and waved to catch Johntie's eye before she joined the game. He tossed the Frisbee to her, an easy one. "You! Ben!" she shouted. The three of them widened into a bigger circle.

That night the smell of burning cane woke her, and she lay sprawled in the center of her bed, luxuriating in the scent drifting through the sliding screen panels that opened onto the upstairs terrace, taking in the air through her mouth, tasting the sweetness. She felt a slight heat in her skin from too much sun, warmest across her cheekbones and shoulders and in a tight band of skin above her knees. She raised her knees so that her thighs opened and she felt the air move between her legs.

Her body felt good to her in the dark, it felt strong and substantial. Was she gaining weight? Cor used to exhort her to gain weight. "Thin. You're too thin," was what he used to say. "You're too thin and you're too much." Like a joke at first, but then he said it too often. She knew what he meant, though, and she would try to get fat—and soft and calm and less talky and less intense. Because that was what he really meant.

She lay still, willing herself to sleep again. What had she been dreaming about? Where had she been? Back in New York, back in the quiet old apartment with its views: Central Park to the west, rooftops to the south, and the gilded domes of St. Nicholas below their bedroom windows.

In her dreams, she was never here. Before, wherever she had lived, a kind of dream geography had always existed concurrently, consistent and detailed, bearing the same name as the place she was in, even when there was very little outward similarity. In the years she had lived in New York City, she had dreamed of Manhattan as a place with enormous dry cliffs on the east. Off the tip of the Battery was a headland with hidden coves and beaches. In dreams she took Benjamin to this beach. In dreams, she drove her little Porsche for hours along Manhattan's cliffs. South Florida, with its long, narrow beach, endless citrus groves, and inland swamps, had not yet made an impression on her subconscious. *In my dreams I haven't even arrived here yet*, she thought.

She heard a noise on the terrace, as if someone had rapped once with a knuckle on the glass, or as if a clay pot had clicked against another. She stopped breathing and held her head rigidly off the bed so that sounds would not be obstructed by the pillows, but the night was quiet and reassuring. The thin gauze curtains stirred, yet no shadow moved against them. Was it possible for someone to climb up to the terrace? The building had smooth stucco sides, with no handholds. There was no way for anyone to climb up, unless he carried a ladder, and who would come so prepared? There were more obvious ways of getting into the house.

She lay still, thinking of various means of entry. The front door could be forced, of course, or the lock could be picked. The kitchen window that faced the lane was vulnerable when its two glass louvers were open. Someone could drive a car right up to the kitchen window, climb up on the hood of the car, and work the screen off, or cut it out of its frame, then slide through, between the horizontal panels of glass. But those panels were operated only by a mechanism inside the kitchen, and she always checked to see that they were open no more than an inch or two before she went to bed.

The triple-locked sliding glass doors that led from the living room to the deck at the back of the house could probably be lifted right off their frames with the right tools and some leverage. That would be noisy though. She had close neighbors in the row of town houses.

Wouldn't it be easier to come in the daytime, she asked an imaginary intruder, and simply say, "I'm the mailman"? Or the water meter man, the Tupperware lady, the exterminator? No, too late to play the role of the exterminator. A man calling himself an exterminator had come last week. She had gladly let him in to rout out the jungle-size cockroaches she had encountered on their mutual nightly patrols, hers and theirs, and after the panicky side-stepping dances they had performed in the dark to avoid each other. Let a dozen exterminators announce themselves at her door. There was a fifty-fifty chance she'd fall for anything. There were some days when everybody looked suspicious to her, and some days when she thought everybody was just who they said they were.

There was another noise, farther away, closer to the canal, and she relaxed. There were always night noises here. What she had heard might have been a jumping fish. When it slapped the water, a fish could make the tinkling sound that she had at first mistaken for flower pots chinking together. She had not learned yet what bird it was that sometimes hooted before dawn in the cactus-strewn field across the canal, but it could have been that bird sending out a single brittle note.

Or it was nothing—nothing to get alarmed about. A natural nighttime noise. Or her own apprehension. Paranoia. She touched her wrist. Cor had given her a bracelet once, one of their joke presents to each other—a silver "medic" bracelet from Tiffany's, with *PARANOIA* engraved on it. Did she still have that bracelet? Not likely. She was sure she had left it behind with all the other trinkets, all the other toys.

They had given each other such funny presents. They had rarely actually needed anything, so they had to think of crazy things to mark gift-giving occasions. She had asked for a janitor's bucket once, seriously. She had seen one in the basement service room of the apartment building in New York, where Benjamin's tricycle was stored. On the occasion of her next birthday or anniversary or whatever, when Cor asked her what she wanted, she said, "A professional janitor's bucket." It became another family joke although she asked for it again and again. Then, for their seventh anniversary, Cor actually went to the Madison Avenue Hardware and bought her one. It sat on three wheels and had two wooden wringers. Cor demonstrated how she could step on a pedal and make the wringers move. "It's a wonderful device," she had said. "I've always wanted one."

Yet she had never felt as if she had everything she wanted.

Benjamin was asleep in his room at the other end of the hall. She could hear him expelling little puffs of sound.

If someone did get into the house at night, would she sense it immediately, or would she lie there, with no intimations of danger? Would she hear a footstep, a groping hand? Would a stranger stumble in the dark over the collection of beach paraphernalia at the front door? Would he be able to navigate the booby traps that sat on the stairs waiting for transport up or down—toys, clean towels, books?

What would she grab as a weapon?

Perhaps she should get out of bed and patrol the house, walk around and touch the doors and windows, so that she could sleep again. If she still couldn't sleep, then she would turn on the small television set at the foot of her bed and watch an old movie. That was better than pills, better than hot milk, better than a glass of brandy. In the city, she and Cormack had seen few films, only the ones people talked about or recommended. Here, she watched movies that she had never seen in her old Manhattan life, and some she had never heard of.

"My life is a Charles Bronson festival," she said to Benjamin, even though the little boy was not allowed to stay up and watch the thrillers that one local station featured. In fact, he would have to wait until he was at least twenty years old, she told him, before he could stay up and watch the scene where the bad guys come with their automatic rifles and shoot up Charles Bronson's crop of watermelons. She didn't intend to interpose herself often between Ben and reality. Even now, living this isolated life, she tried to leave a space around him in which he operated by his own rules, a space she had longed to possess for herself as a child. She gave him as much autonomy as he could handle, but the worst comic books, the worst movies, the brutal ones, were censored. He was not old enough for violence presented in such ordinary guises.

Benjamin declared that he would never be happy until he'd seen the bad guys shooting the watermelons. "Boy," he said, and his eyes glowed.

Another film actor whose movies were new to her was Clint Eastwood. She liked Bronson's silence better than Eastwood's, but something in the roles both actors played appealed to her. There was always a moment that she recognized as a recurring one in her own life, a moment when by their example she thought she should be able to meet the forces that acted on her life with a matching energy of her own.

"To live outside of society," Mercer said to Benjamin, "you have to be really honest." But Benjamin had no idea how close they were to living outside. They were as much drifters in this anon-

ymous town of drifters and tourists as Clint Eastwood was in a frontier community with a gun on
his hip.

The curtains moved again, billowing away from
the sliding glass panels that led from Mercer's bedroom to the balcony.

How would Charles Bronson deal with an intruder?

First of all, he would not lie there wondering
who was downstairs, she thought. He would probably guess the identity of the intruder, maybe in-
truders, at the first muffled sound. Something
would give them away. He would have known,
anyway, that they were never going to leave
him alone. They would persist in persecuting him
because they suspected that somewhere at the
limits of his passiveness, there was a moment
when they both might blaze higher. A footfall in
a dark room, a hand on the latch—all clear to
Charles Bronson. His eyes are narrowed slits. He
is wide-awake.

He tenses his muscles, those fine muscles he has
created for just such an emergency by endlessly
pumping iron and chopping wood, and slides out
of bed like a shadow to pull on his tight jeans and
black turtleneck sweater, an outfit that becomes
him. No, rewrite the scene: He is already dressed
in jeans and dark sweater, lying there waiting and
ready. He goes downstairs, in full view of anyone
who might be hovering outside the glass doors at
the back, yet he's a shadow on the wall.

He slips through the house without passing in

front of the windows. This is the trickiest part since only a few feet of wall in the living room are not glass, exposed to the night and to any determined watcher. With her first paycheck, Mercer vowed, she would buy heavy curtains to pull across the expanse of glass.

What would he do next? Oh, he'd know. He would have a plan, a weapon. Or he'd improvise, sometimes with unexpected and bloody results . . . or actually maybe he did expect those bloody results. She was putting herself to sleep. The thought of an intruder was becoming tedious, and the perfumed air lulled her back into dreams.

Mercer slept again, until the sun lit the fields across the canal, sending insects spinning into the heat and out over the water, where silver-sided mullet jumped for their breakfast. This time the clock radio woke her with soft South Florida rock. Nowhere else in the country could you hear so much McCartney, so much Rod Stewart. Old Kinks. You could still hear "Layla" and "Sail on Sailor." It was like turning on the Sixties again.

The breeze lifted the curtain and the sun streamed in. Things seemed so normal that when she stepped out on the terrace to see what the morning was like, she was not alarmed at all to find a fish under a climbing vine, gutted and cool on a broad palm frond as if it had been served up from the night sea, its scales silver and gray, its enormous black eye staring sightlessly at the sky.

African pompano, she thought. Johntie must

have fished far out last night, toward the Bahamas. What a nice gift to find on such a fine morning. When she wondered how he had gotten it up to her balcony, the question did not bother her at all: She supposed he must have lobbed it up, faultlessly, like his Frisbee.

CHAPTER TWO

"Mer-CER! Mommy!"

Mercer, carrying the fish on its leaf as if she were bearing a platter, came in from the balcony just as Benjamin, pajama-clad, burst into her room.

"Ma! There's a bird flying into the glass door downstairs." He hit the bed and bounced on his knees until she put on her bathrobe. They hurried down together.

"Look!" Benjamin's voice was high. Although she did not glimpse the fast approach of the bird, Mercer saw it fall stunned to the deck.

"Poor thing. Why doesn't it realize it can't get through? Why does it keep making the same mistake?"

She and Benjamin slid the panel open and ran outside, but the bird had disappeared. They pulled Ben's rubber float across the deck and propped it against the glass door as a warning marker. It was bright blue and reached shoulder high.

"Okay, that should do it," Mercer said. "I wonder if it was a bird that hit my window just before dawn? Something made that same kind of noise and woke me up." They watched for a few minutes, ready to wave the bird off if it should return, but it did not come back. "How about some breakfast?" Mercer asked. "I'll race you getting dressed and then we'll have breakfast outside."

Mercer had bought a bamboo table and two chairs at the local Goodwill store, and had placed them out beyond the end of the deck, on the seawall, where she and Benjamin breakfasted. From there they could look down the canal to the waterway and see the charter boats and the drift boats setting out for Briney Inlet, the nearest open passage to the sea. Mercer loved to watch the early morning light over the water. Just behind their house, across the canal, was empty land, waiting for the inevitable developer. For the moment, cactus and palmetto claimed the key, and on some mornings a leggy pompous blue heron walked around the field, as tall as a man.

They sat companionably over breakfast, Mercer with her hands wrapped around a cup of coffee, Ben redistributing raisins through his cereal in an equitable manner.

This is all I really want, she thought. *To sit across the table from my child and watch him pour milk over his cereal. That's really all.*

"What a clear morning," she said to Benjamin, and they both looked up into the inverted blue bowl of the sky. As they looked, a Frisbee sailed over the roof of their house and hesitated in the center of the sky before it floated down toward the table.

"Yay!" shouted Benjamin, falling out of his chair; he almost caught it.

Johntie came around the end of the house

laughing, pushing his way through the overgrown path. His eyes were so full of light that the color suffused the iris and flashed back the same sapphire blue of the morning.

Johntie was a solitary man. He had a little yellow Fiat that he took fanatic care of, he fished with single-minded intensity, and he tended a small patch of marijuana behind his cottage. He lived with the simplicity cultivated by the children of the Sixties who grew up in comfortable homes with well-to-do parents. "We don't need much," they said, not knowing how much was needed. Johntie had told her that deafness was not the impairment most people imagined it to be. The impairment could be minimized if—"if the deaf could go to the kind of schools my father sent me to." And if they were bright and gifted as well, Mercer added silently, after seeing some of his camera work. Now his only ambitions were to fish and "take care of my head," which, she guessed, meant he dealt a little grass on the side.

Mercer thanked him for the fish he had left for them, and heard the fish's story: How it was hooked; how it fought; how the shimmer of blues and greens on its side changed to silver as it lay on the deck; how its eye transfixed the young man—"He looked at me!"—so that Johntie almost jerked away, almost let his prize thump its way across the deck and back into the sea. All this Johntie communicated in his own animated mixture of speech and pantomime, with Mercer and Benjamin as his attentive audience.

"Hey, I almost forgot." Mercer tapped her

watch. "It's time for school." She sent Benjamin to collect his books and his lunchbox.

"Can you give me a ride to the dock?" Johntie signalled. "My car is kaput." He gave a fading raspberry sound to describe a dying engine, and she smiled. "Yes."

"We'd better get going," she called to Benjamin. "Pile in."

Benjamin jumped in the front seat, rattling his lunchbox while Johntie carefully lowered his fishing rods into the backseat and held them upright so that they went up and out of the window. Mercer thought how normal the three of them must look, setting out for the day in the conservative secondhand Plymouth that was nearly as old as Benjamin. She backed out of the driveway, wondering if the house looked safe, anonymous? It was an attractive enough place because of its location, but it was little more than a box with glass at the front and back. At least it was one remove from traditional Florida architecture, which was based on the trailer, Mercer had decided. Small homes looked like single trailers, larger ones like two trailers. Split-level houses looked like two and a half trailers. When the building boom began on this coast, contractors must have looked awfully close at hand for inspiration.

Her house was one of a line of town houses on a canal that turned sharply off the Intracoastal Waterway. A pleasant living room at the back of the house led to an open deck that reached to the seawall. Upstairs, there were two bedrooms. Hers, with a narrow balcony hanging above the canal, showed the broad sweep of the Waterway if she leaned on the railing and looked to her right, and a high view of the sunset in the other direction.

Driving the few blocks to Benjamin's school, she was held up briefly on First Street by a passing freight train. The town was so small that a railroad ran right through it. It was a single track; the cars went north in the daytime and south at night. Wherever you were in the town, you could hear the whistle of the trains, unless you lived west of the cold chain of lights that marked Interstate Highway 95.

Waiting for the train to go by, Johntie spelled words on his fingers to Benjamin, and Benjamin patiently spelled them again for Mercer, putting his small hand against the dash in her line of vision. They were learning the manual alphabet, Benjamin quickly and Mercer more laboriously. "T-r-a-i-n," Benjamin spelled. Mercer took her right hand off the steering wheel and repeated the word while they waited for the train gates to go up.

The yellow stone Spanish-mission style building that was Benjamin's school was only a few blocks away. It had not been difficult to get Benjamin into school, as it would have been if he were older and a transfer student. Mercer McCormack, Mrs. Benjamin Cormack McCormack III, had become *M. Ramsey*, someone quite different, complete with a new Social Security card. She had enrolled Benjamin Ramsey McCormack in first grade as *Ben Ramsey*. "We'll use my old name while we're here together," she told him. The explanation was acceptable to Benjamin. He acquired a new health record in much the same way. Mercer simply had him inoculated all over again, using the new name to create a new record.

The busy pediatrician shrugged. "It can't hurt."

At the school office, she explained Benjamin's lack of a school record. "He has been in an alternative kindergarten," she told Mr. Goode, the principal. "My friends and I ran it—a cooperative nursery school and kindergarten. We concentrated on creativity." She went on to describe further the philosophy of the school. "We didn't keep formal records," she finished. "We just didn't have time."

So Benjamin became a first-grader at Briney Breezes Elementary School.

"You're not going to believe this," Benjamin told her after the first day of school. "There's writing on the wall in the boys' bathroom, and guess what? They know *that word* here too."

She answered him reassuringly, as if it were a sign of continuity, as if she were saying that the two of them were not really living at the end of a dusty road in a strange Southern town. "They know that word everywhere, sweetheart."

She drove him to school in the mornings, and in the afternoons watched for him to come dawdling home through lanes shaded by ficus trees, past the neat bungalows and manicured lawns of Century Acres. "Do you have to be one hundred years old to live there?" Mercer had asked her neighbor Susan. Then Benjamin would cross the highway with the other children under the school crossing guard's watchful eye, and pass along the row of small shops on Main Street. These included, Mercer had noted, The New York Clothing Shop, Dan's New and Used Furniture, Dora's Home Cooking, and the Liberty News Stand, with a printed admonition over the door: "Thank God You Live in a Capitalist Country." The safety of a small town had a price—smallness, conservatism, resistance to change.

Mercer practiced the walk home from school with Benjamin for the first few weeks. The only hard bit seemed to be the railroad crossing because Ben had to learn to look both ways, even if the signals were not down. After that, the walk through Century Acres was easy enough. She found that she did not worry inordinately about Benjamin when he was away from her. It was part of the reliance she was placing in small town life. She believed that if a child really needed help, another adult would come to his rescue, as she herself would aid a child in distress. And the retirees in Century Acres seemed friendly.

One day, on one of their trial runs, Mercer and Benjamin came to the gates that marked the end of the development. The last two bungalows faced the avenue at an angle, and on the small green lawns stood two black cannons, pointing at the outside world. "Are they real?" asked Benjamin.

"They look real," answered Mercer.

An old lady came out of one of the villas to speak to them. "Don't climb on the cannon, little boy," she called as she approached.

"Oh, he won't. He's just interested," Mercer said.

Mollified, the woman told them a little about the cannons. The Century Acres community had built the two cannons and set them up as part of the town's bicentennial celebration. "They really work," the woman claimed, "and they make a terrible noise. We use carbide for the charge," she explained. "It's not dangerous or messy. This is an exact model of the naval cannon at Fort Ticonderoga, young man." She abruptly turned her attention entirely on Benjamin. "If you can tell me who won the American Revolution, I'll let you set one of these off, all by yourself."

Benjamin came to attention. "The Americans won!" he shouted.

"Very good. I want you to remember that. It's very important to have a good report card. And I want you to remember all the poor children who don't have cable television."

Poor baby, he looks so puzzled, Mercer thought, deciding that the old woman was wandering a bit. "Can we walk you across the avenue?" she offered. "We are going that way."

"Yes, thank you. I am going to sit on a bench in the park behind the shopping center," the elderly lady said. "I like to sit there and watch the trucks unload. Isn't it wonderful? Every truck has something in it."

They escorted the woman across the thoroughfare, then continued home. "Do you think she will let me fire off the cannon, Ma?" Benjamin asked.

"Mm-hmm. Maybe on the Fourth of July. And

I'll tell you what—one more practice run and I'll let you try coming home from school by yourself."

Beyond the everyday sort of hazard—splinters, burrs, scraped knees—nothing very terrible could happen to this child, or if it did, surely it would happen when she was at his side. And she was prepared to do whatever had to be done. So she allowed him to climb trees, fish off the seawall, and walk home from school by himself. She tried to worry only in a normal, everyday way.

Sometimes, if Benjamin was late coming home from school, there was a little moment of tension. But what was she worried about? That he would be kidnapped? He had already been kidnapped— by Cor, by herself, and by Quinn. She had become very good at it. Back in New York, she had always known Benjamin's schedule. On any weekday she could be at the school door by three o'clock or on Saturday mornings in the playground by the museum at ten. Very cool, better each time. Cor's detective had talked all the way back to New York, kindly pointing out to her where she had gone wrong, giving her the information she needed for a final successful flight. And this time they had been safe for months and months.

The crossing bell sounded and the gates lifted. Mercer pressed her foot on the gas and bumped gently over the railroad tracks.

"I need a pencil," announced Benjamin as they pulled into the school yard.

"Why didn't you think of that before we left home?" Mercer asked him as she scrabbled in the debris on the dashboard. "There must be one somewhere. Here, how's this?" She held up a ball-point pen, but it came apart in her hands. The little spring flew out, and she tossed the parts back.

"We're not allowed pens," said Benjamin.

"Check under the seat," Mercer commanded. "Look, there's one—two—a whole nest of pencils."

"I'm late! That's the last bell!" Benjamin kicked at the door of the car and struggled with his books and pencils and lunchbox.

"It was the train that made us late," she said. "Have a good day."

He turned and ran without a backward glance, and Mercer watched him go, loving the small jean-clad behind, the straight back, the skinny neck, the shining brown thatch of hair. Then she drove back to Main Street and headed for the marina.

While Johntie was extricating his rods and tackle box, she scribbled quickly on a piece of paper, "I won't be able to give you a ride tomorrow—I think I'm going to get a *job*."

He read over her shoulder as she finished the note and nodded. "Okay, it's cool."

She could always understand his speech if she knew that they were talking about the same thing. Sometimes, when he changed the subject abruptly, he left her behind. Now he said, "Good luck," and smiled at her. She smiled back at him, nodding. Communicating with Johntie involved so much of one's self. She had noticed that both she and Benjamin had begun to employ body language, mime, rolling eyes, shrugs, much more than speech alone—and were probably overdoing it, she thought. She had spoken to Benjamin twice recently with such exaggerated facial gestures that he had howled, "Mer-CER! I'm not deaf."

"Good luck to you too," she said to Johntie. "Catch a big one!" She measured out a two-foot-long fish and then stretched out her arms another foot. He laughed and shook his head. What a beautiful boy, she thought.

After dropping Johntie at the marina, she was nearer the shore road than the highway, so she crossed the bridge and drove upcounty on A1A, the two-lane road that ran along the water. It was slower, but she had plenty of time, almost half an hour before her interview. She had a feeling she would get this job. The description in the paper and the preliminary telephone conversations had been encouraging. "I now want to work desperately, as desperately as I want a drink on a hot day." That was a line from a Chekhov play she'd been in when she was in college. Should she use the line at her interview? She tried it a couple of times, dramatically, and laughed at herself.

The bridge at Briney Inlet was high enough to give her a view of the Intracoastal Waterway to the west. On the other side was the open sea, pale green today, and so clear that she could see the reef showing black under the surface a few yards offshore. Farther out, the Gulf Stream unwound like a distant highway on the sea.

A day like this made her feel good. What she had to guard against were those long evenings when she felt alone and afraid and played the Beatles over and over, listening for clues, drinking brandy until the decanter was empty.

Obviously life here was going to be what many of her friends would call being buried alive. Well, that was what she wanted. She would bury herself—in raising her child, finding a job, reading, growing tomatoes, jogging on the beach. Buried. Alive. But doing things. Managing her daily life, shoring up her real strength against the appearance of the real enemy. That was the most anyone could do, more than many people managed.

Look at Lenin, she thought. Waiting to come to power, what did he do? He spent his time sharpening pencils. Someone, his brother or his wife, had said that he sharpened them with a sort of special tenderness, so that the letters written with them came out like delicate threads. Very nice, but she felt that she had to do real things, like working at a job and chauffering Benjamin to softball games. And Napoleon. Wasn't she using her time more profitably than Napoleon, who had spent hours of every day during his last exile taking long baths? Long, long baths, with a book propped before him. . . .

Getting a job was a step in the right direction. It would be good for her to work hard, to fall asleep exhausted at ten o'clock. And besides, there was the money. The money she had brought with her, the money her father had left her, would not last much longer.

In addition, she needed some contact with other people—casual office friendships, someone to lunch with, someone to ask for the name of a doctor or a dentist. That would be enough. Then she would know a handful of people—those she worked with, the postman, the librarian, the druggist who put aside the Sunday *New York Times* for her. She wanted no more involvement than that. She had been pushed and pulled by others for a long time. She had used wasteful, extravagant amounts of energy trying to leave and leaving. Being married to Cormack had burned her out, especially the last year of being wife and adversary at the same time.

Now she would bury herself in a life that was at least all her own. And if *they* tracked her down, bothered her—she smiled, in her assertive mood, at the childish, querulous word—if they bothered her, she would simply do whatever she had to do to brush them off. Get rid of them. You and me, Charles Bronson. Push them, drown them, shoot them, run them over, set traps for them, tap them with an iron bar. Bludgeon was the word she was searching for. What a word! You and me, Charlie.

"Ridin' out from Memphis . . ." she sang into the wind. Thunderheads were building up out over the water, and the wind freshened. She felt wonderful. The job, whatever it entailed, was as good as hers already. She would bulldoze her way past the interviewer. Experience be damned. She would simply claim to be able to do whatever the position demanded. She could be quick-witted when she tried. By the time she had to deliver, she would have mastered whatever skill was required. How did she know she could? Well, she'd simply demand it of herself.

She was going to get this job. She was going to pay the rent on the house by the canal that was close to the solace of water and birds and leaping fish. Ben would fish and swim and learn to tie sailors' knots and hit a baseball. She would manage this thing, giving Ben a safe and ordinary life, and she'd do it as well as it could be done.

The morning sun hit the sea, glittering on the surface in a pattern of diamonds. The salty, sun-hardened air rocketed through the car as she sped northward to the next bridge connecting the narrow strip of coast with the mainland. She punched the radio and shook her head when she heard the Beach Boys singing "Don't Worry Baby": The anxiety song of all time, the national anthem of anxious sufferers leaning toward the future with all their strength.

"Hey, hey," she prayed. "Amen."

CHAPTER THREE

In the year after her husband told her that he was in love with another woman, Mercer McCormack had made many wonderful dishes, but she decided that tonight's dinner would surpass them all.

She lit the candles in the Queen Anne candlestick long before she expected Cormack home and watched them burn for a few seconds to savor the effect. The branched candlestick had belonged to her grandmother and was almost the only thing Mercer owned from the house in which she had finished growing up. Everything else was still in that house, even the bed she had slept in as a child. The blankets on that bed had been woven by her grandmother from wool from the family's sheep. Now Mercer's stepmother inhabited that house, and everything in it was hers.

The flame flickered on the candles. The table, set for two, warmed under the soft light. The silver gleamed, the flowers in the center of the table were just what she'd wanted. It had been extremely satisfying to create such a bouquet. She had walked up and down Madison Avenue that morning, mixing greenery from various shops, long

sprays of blossoming wild blackberry, fat white
peonies, and lacy alyssum.

After the flowers were done, she had left her
own car in the garage and called for Cormack's
limo. Why not? she had thought. The limo was
billed to Cormack's office, but it was really for
family use. She couldn't understand why she
hadn't used it more often. It was a luxurious convenience. James might as well be chauffering her
around as circling the New York Athletic Club,
waiting for Cormack to emerge from his squash
game.

She called James in the Bronx, and he drove
down and picked her up at her front door. He
transported her to the west side of town, to the
market area on Ninth Avenue where he guided
the car slowly along behind her as she went from
butcher to greengrocer, loading the car with bags
and boxes and jars: Sweet butter, fragrant coffee
beans, pale and dark greens for salad. Through the
rest of the afternoon she chopped and minced and
blended and boned, happily at work alone in the
kitchen.

She had given the others—the cook and Mrs.
Donovan, the housekeeper—the rest of the weekend off, all but Marie-Theresa, the au pair, who
lived in Benjamin's wing of the rambling old apartment and took him to the park in the afternoon
and listened for the little boy to wake at night. The
two of them were there now, getting five-year-old
Benjamin ready for his bath. With the kitchen to
herself, Mercer prepared the entire anniversary

meal, from the clear golden consommé to Cor's favorite childhood dessert, tipsy cake.

She imagined her husband's arrival, imagined his face when he glanced into the dining room, pictured a smile slowly transforming his features. What did she think she was trying to do?

She almost answered, "Make Cor happy," except that she knew her efforts were just as likely to enrage him as to please him. But she wanted to remind him of how well she did all this—the flowers, the food, the air of celebration. Remind him of the warm comfort of domesticity. Stick the three of them, Cor and Mercer and Benjamin, back into the sweet gummy custard of family life.

Yet . . . was this really the way to do it? She squeezed a lemon and searched for an egg. Mixing the salad dressing vigorously, beating the oil to a smooth blend, she winced when a drop of lemon juice ran across a small cut on the side of her thumb. During the past few months she had constantly discovered small wounds on her hands. Nicks, bruised knuckles. She could never remember how she got them; she never struck out at Cormack. When she was transported by anger, her gestures became wilder, more random. She swung her fists against the frames of doors as she passed through, sliced the heel of her hand open on the edge of the library table. She supposed that anger made her clumsy. Sometimes she stopped in mid-argument to pick at a newly flayed piece of skin on her finger. How had it happened? Once, screaming at Cor and trying to open a wine bottle at the same time, she drilled the corkscrew right into the center of her hand. She hardly noticed.

On their wedding anniversary a year ago, Cor had taken her to the theater and out to dinner, and had told her that he thought he was in love with someone else. Who had it been? An actress. Was it the actress that time? She only remembered the occasion. She had been wearing her velvet dinner suit and his grandmother's pearls.

"It's my bad luck to be married to a romantic," she complained to her friends Sarah and Ina and Grace. "He falls in love as easily as catching a cold."

"A romantic!" they'd laughed at her. "There's another name for it. Wasn't his father a famous philanderer? You're the romantic, Mercy."

This anniversary marked a year of trying, really trying, on her part. She had thought of ways to mend the marriage, ways of holding them together. She offered to jog with him.

"And if you want to entertain more, we'll do it," she said. "Or do you want to do politics?"

"I don't want it," Cor said to everything. "What I really want is to be left alone."

"But I thought this was what you wanted," said Mercer, waving her hand around the library in the Fifth Avenue apartment they'd inherited from his family and striking the sharp edge of the library table with the heel of her hand. "You never told me that this was not what you wanted!"

She missed Watergate. For a long time Watergate had held them together, united them. It gave a shape and focus to their lives. They passed sections of *The New York Times* back and forth over the breakfast table, and she looked forward all through the day to the evening news, which they watched together in the library with their feet up. Watergate added content to their lives. Mercer memorized sections of the White House tapes as they were revealed to the public and could perform them in credible accents. Both followed up newspaper coverage by reading serious reportage and analyses in the news magazines. Mercer worked like an anxious student at mastering the constitutional aspects of the country's crisis. She had not pursued a subject so thoroughly since Benjamin was a baby and she had spent many hours at home and sitting in the park, watching him sleep while she read.

In those months of being the immobilized mother of an infant, she had pored over books on gardening, memorizing the plantings in the formal gardens of England and Europe. Sometimes she felt she knew places she had never seen better than she knew the places she had actually lived in, better than she knew Cormack's family home in Connecticut. She believed she knew the way through the maze at Hampton Court. She believed she knew how the avenue of lime trees leading to the river at Sissinghurst would look in any season of the year. Well, she thought, stirring the cake batter, it was strange how you knew some things exhaustively, and then they were over, and they never mattered anymore. She had never made a real garden. Watergate was dead and buried. She missed it.

Mercer left things in the last stages of preparation in the kitchen and went to the other wing of the apartment to watch Benjamin have his bath and get ready for bed. Marie-Theresa was waiting for her with laughter.

"When I was running Benjamin's bath," she said, "the pipes were making all sorts of noises." The plumbing in this rambling old Fifth Avenue warren had not been renewed as often as the gilt in the lobby. "Benjamin said to me, '*Quelle chanson est-ce que c'est?*'" Marie-Theresa laughed and handed Benjamin, wrapped papoose-fashion in his towel, over to Mercer to hold while the girl turned down his bed. Mercer bent over her son, snuffling his thatch of damp hair, breathing the pure clean scent of the child and catching his warm breath against her cheek.

"Can I wait up for Daddy?"

"Daddy and I will come in later," she promised him.

"Even if I'm asleep?"

"Even if."

She shifted him in her lap and gathered him up to move over to the rocking chair. She was not sure to what degree the emotional ups and downs between herself and Cor affected Benjamin. Sometimes she thought the little boy had such a fixed idea of them as parents that not even the foolish things they had done in the past year could dislodge their icons: At other times he seemed extraordinarily sensitive to their emotional vibrations.

Last spring he had gone for days without voluntarily speaking to them. He seemed to become more compulsive, more insistent that the routines of the nursery wing be followed without any variation. She was worried that their unhappiness was driving the child into a self-absorbed shell, while at the same time—in the state she was in then— she had used even Benjamin's silence as a weapon. *I used every weapon I had,* she thought as she rocked her son back and forth, running her fingers through his wet brown curls.

"Look at what you're doing to Benjamin," she had accused Cormack. "He's so quiet. He doesn't chatter anymore, he doesn't ask his questions. He has hardly spoken in weeks."

"He's all right," said Cor, but nevertheless he brought up the possibility of seeing a child psychologist.

"You mean, he should learn to cope with our problems, with the help of an expert, if necessary? That's a rotten suggestion," she declared.

Mercer remembered, hugged Benjamin, and rocked harder, smiling. She was picturing the day at the breakfast table when Benjamin had sighed a huge sigh of relief and looked up grinning from his scrambled eggs. "I did it," he said to them.

"Did what, sweetie?"

"I counted to a million by ones."

Mercer and Cormack stared at each other over his head. "Why, that's wonderful, Skipper," Cormack said. "I don't know anybody else who has ever done that." He buttered a piece of toast and laid it on the boy's plate.

"How long did it take?" Mercer asked him.

"Oh, a long time. Since we went to the circus."

"That long?" Mercer looked back at Cor, relieved and amazed.

"I don't know anyone else with your present understanding of a million," Cor told him. "You may find it very useful one of these days."

"What do you mean?" Mercer asked him.

"Just that there may be something special in Grandmother McCormack's will for Benjamin. He has Grandfather's name, you know."

"But not millions," she said. "I don't believe it." But Cormack was again congratulating Benjamin on his achievement.

She never did hear, or was never told, what was in Grandmother McCormack's will.

"Do you remember when you counted to a million?" she asked Benjamin, hugging his damp, towel-wrapped body and rocking him. "You counted right through the war."

Mercer placed the salt on the table in open cut-glass salt dishes, the same kind her grandmother had always had on her table. One took a pinch of salt between two fingers, then rubbed the fingers together above the plate to distribute the salt. Some guests disliked the country manners of taking a pinch of salt from a common dish, but she liked it. Oh, wasn't it time for Cormack to come home?

She looked at herself in the mirror above the mantel. A tall, slender blue-eyed woman gazed coolly back. She rubbed the skin over her cheekbone with a finger. Too dry? Stretched too tight? No, she looked okay, she looked the way Cormack liked her to look. She was wearing makeup. He liked women to wear makeup. She had released her hair from its usual band and pulled it around so that it shadowed her jawbone, softened her rather angular face. An application of rose color across her cheeks made her look flushed and brought a glow to her eyes. It could be a nice evening, she thought. We could talk about all the good times. It was strange how the mind wouldn't hold any strong feelings for very long—anger, fear, sorrow. They kept slipping away. She had been angry at Cormack for a long time, but she found it impossible to be angry consistently. So much of each day was taken up with just living; she always found herself slipping back into civil, wifely routines. *Well, after all*, she thought, *I was brought up to be somebody's wife*. Was that the sound of the front door closing?

He dropped his briefcase and papers in the hall and advanced as far as the double doors that opened into the dining room, just far enough to glance into the room. He looked at the candles and the enormous bouquet in the center of the table, then at her. In the silence she could hear the sound of Cormack gritting his teeth.

He walked off abruptly in the direction of his dressing room, leaving Mercer to pace back and forth from the dining room to the butler's pantry, pulling the drapes, picking up fallen blackberry petals from the table, warming the consommé again, chilling the two bottles of champagne again. She was beginning to repeat the activities of the afternoon, but with a slight frenzy that made her clumsy. She calmed herself with an incantation she had recently learned from Grace, who said it whenever her teenage son wrecked a car: "Everything I know about him, and much that I don't know about him, leads me to believe that it was inevitable for him to do what he has just done." Repeating Grace's canticle kept her from being astonished at anything Cormack did or said.

Since Cormack was now home, she told herself, it must be time to uncork the champagne. It was not easy, but she worked at the cork with her thumbs and finally it came shooting out, ricocheting off the mirror. She poured the wine into her own glass and then crossed to the other side of the table to fill Cormack's. Standing at his empty chair, she lifted his glass in a silent toast and sipped from it. Then she said, "You aren't drinking, darling. Won't you drink a toast with me to mark our anniversary?"

She walked back to the other side of the table and lifted her own glass. "I will, love. To Benjamin Cormack McCormack the Third, and his charming and capable wife, Mercer. His attractive and talented wife, Mercer." She couldn't think of two adjectives that went together; she'd have to settle for one. "His dedicated wife, Mercer."

Cormack came back down the hall. In one hand he carried the small portable Sony; his other hand was clenched around the neck of a bottle of Scotch. He angled through one corner of the dining room, heading for the door to the serving pantry.

"There is some ice on the sideboard," she called to him.

"Ummm."

"Will you want something to eat?"

"No."

"Why did you come home, then?"

"To watch the Democratic debate." He passed out of sight.

"Your candidate is going to lose," she said, confidentially, to the empty chair across the table. "I can save you a lot of trouble by telling you that now. He's going to lose. How much money have you given him so far?"

Cormack walked through the dining room again, going in the opposite direction. He was carrying a folded newspaper in his hand, which he shook at her. "If you ever again touch *The Wall Street Journal* before I see it, I'll wring your neck."

"You'll throw me the papers after you've finished with them?" she asked tartly. Domestic fights always sounded like vaudeville, she thought, and she hoped they would not wind up throwing things from the table at each other, because she had labored so long in the kitchen and now she was really hungry.

"You know what I mean." He came over to the table. "Look at this," he said, opening the pages. "It's all marked up *with ink*. 'Read this.' 'Skip this.' 'Notice what Charter stock is doing.' 'Send David a note—they've made him a member of the board.' What the fuck do you think you're doing?"

"I'm trying to save you time. Besides, I know what I'm talking about. I've mastered all that Wall Street talk, I've made a point of doing it. That's so we'll have something to talk about when you come home. It's all you will talk about."

"I've had enough. And please don't tell me the price of gold at the breakfast table. Why don't you sleep late, as I hear other women do?" He threw the paper on a corner of the table and stalked out.

Mercer poured the last of the champagne into her glass and squinted into the bottle. Her mother had been an alcoholic. *And here I am, the alcoholic's daughter, all these years later finding out what's in the bottle. And it is there. It's really there, after all. All those times I asked my mother, why do you drink? And she never said, it makes me feel better, it makes me feel good.*

It occurred to Mercer for the first time that perhaps her parents' marriage had not been so different from her own. She had spent years trying to penetrate their private life, trying to glimpse their secret feelings for each other, but she had never succeeded. Then—and now, for that matter—she had had very little information by which to judge the character of a marriage. What seemed bizarre to her might be an ordinary event. Perhaps many women were cooking anniversary dinners that were destined not to be eaten by their husbands.

Cormack passed through the room again. "Look, Cor," she called to him. "Isn't this a pretty room? Isn't our life better than most? Don't let's lose it all. Oh, I know you want me to be different. I know you like a challenge, even in marriage, and I'm not a challenge."

He paused and looked at her. "You are totally

mistaken if you think I want a challenge. And you are quite enough and more of a challenge than I bargained for, to tell you the truth."

"Then I will try to be less!" she burst out. "I know you don't like talk that's analytical and personal, that who am I, what are we to each other sort of stuff. Well, okay, I don't like it either. It doesn't . . . it doesn't bring clarity. I can drop it. And if you want me to do sports with you, I'll do sports, and if you want me to entertain more, I will. I'll—I'll be perfect. I will. Look, I'll put up a note in my closet where I'll see it every morning: Be Calm, Smile."

He groaned. "Can't you just leave me alone?"

"Do you want me to have a career?" The idea brought a rise of energy, and she spoke with excitement. "I think I could really do something if I tried. You know, have a career, accomplish something."

"What do you want to be, Mercer?"

"I think . . . a landscape gardener."

"A what? For God's sake, Mercer. When did you come up with that?"

"I think I've always . . . I remember when I was very little, before we moved into bigger and bigger houses, we lived in a house with a garden. It was a beautiful garden, half-wild, with a field of those blue—little blue flowers, wild asters? They're weeds, almost, but they're lovely. I always thought I could do that, make a garden. Create a place I would want to be, where others would want to be—"

Cormack interrupted her, leaning over the table

to poke at something in the salad. "What is this?" He fished out the champagne cork.

"Give it to me!" she demanded, half-rising and reaching across the table. "You're not listening to me!" She grabbed the cork, knocking the empty bottle from the table. "And I'll cook your favorite meals," she shouted, "and I'll tell Cook to make just the things you like best. And look, if happiness is what you want, we'll be happy, we can do that. I'll stick with it. I'll really work at it."

"Oh, Mercy, happiness is not your style." Cormack frowned. He took a roll from the table and buttered it. He walked around the room, munching on it, looking down on the traffic on Fifth Avenue and at the dark park beyond. "Can you think of a time when we were really happy? When we were happy and knew it. When we could actually say, now we are happy, at this moment?"

Happy? Oh, yes, she suddenly remembered. "When your grandmother's things arrived."

Cormack's grandmother had grown up in a Rhenish castle in the Hudson Valley, in a large and fabled family, in which each daughter, upon marriage and as a matter of course, was presented by her mother with twelve dozen of everything— every household need, enough to last the lifetime of a marriage: Twelve dozen linen napkins, twelve dozen linen sheets, twelve dozen linen towels, twelve dozen linen pillow cases. In the fourth year of their marriage, Cormack's grandmother died in a Swiss clinic. The disposition of the matriarch's estate would take a year, two years—many years. Meanwhile in the early disbursement of her personal possessions, part of the family linens—wearing like iron and smelling faintly of lavender—had been dispensed to Cormack and Mercer in New York. Packed among the linens, perhaps an oversight, were a number of Cormack's grandmother's nightgowns—fine brushed flannel, voluminous, sprigged with flowers or patterned like old-fashioned wallpaper. Cor chose a design of blue morning glories running up and down a green trellis. Mercer picked one with tiny pink and blue flowers scattered on a field of white. So soft, so warm. Rosy from their bath, they pulled the gowns on over their heads. Their damp hair curled on the high round lace-edged collars, their wrists stuck out of the buttoned cuffs. As they raced for bed, Mercer saw Cor's strong pale ankles flash like signals leading her pell-mell down the long hall. "We were happy then," she reminded him.

Cor looked at her with exasperation. "I'm talking about planned happiness, programmed happiness. I don't mean little epiphanies that arrive unannounced. I don't want to leave my life to chance. What I mean by happiness is deciding what I want and getting it."

Perhaps we're just too different, she thought. Outwardly we seem like the same kind of people, wanting the same kind of things. She had tried to adopt his attitude—that emotions interfered with the smooth daily operation of one's life. *I haven't been properly programmed*, she thought, *even though I was sent to the right schools*.

She looked at Cormack closely, wishing she had put in her contact lenses. The candlelight smoothed out the tight lines around his mouth and made his face look like a mask. His dark hair, his hundred-dollar haircut, fit his head like a helmet —Cormack looked like a robot. His hard green eyes never changed their focus, his mouth was a tight line—an efficient design. Robots need not be designed to smile; it would have no technical application.

He picked a mushroom out of the salad bowl and then put it back. "I'm going to look in on Benjamin. I'll take a drop of champagne when you get that other bottle open."

"Certainly," she said with great civility to his chair, which was empty again. She took the bottle she was wrestling with and pulled the cork out with her teeth, then filled Cor's glass and her own. She went around to Cor's side of the table and lifted his glass. "Here's to marriage. To love and companionship and so on and so on." She drank half of the glass in a single gulp and refilled it. "Which brings me to the question I really wanted to discuss tonight . . . which is . . . How are we to live now? With all my preparation, I don't know. With all the advice my parents gave me, with all the stuff I learned in school, with all the reading I do, I just can't find out. Not by example or precept." She sat down in her chair again, holding the heavy green bottle in her lap.

"I hate the sound of sighing." Cormack was standing in the doorway once more. He came into the dining room and sank into his chair, picking at the plate of caviar. He set the open bottle of

Scotch in the middle of the table, pushing the bouquet of flowers to the side. "Mercer," he said, "I think I want to be married to someone else."

She turned a blind face to him, but he knew counterfeit attention when he saw it. He waited until he had her real attention, then continued to talk. Mercer listened for a name. She waited and listened, and finally he spoke one. It was not the name she was expecting to hear.

However, it was a name anyone who read the gossip columns, anyone who read *W* and *Vogue* and the "People" column in *The New York Times*, would know. Marrying her would be like marrying the president's widow, or one of the Ford women. She was rich, of course. And it was old money; her grandfather had been a governor, her grandmother had been both a Chase and a Phillips, and her father was a congressman with presidential ambitions. What was more, the woman had a title from a previous marriage. Princess, countess, duchess, something improbable. Mercer picked carefully among her bits of information, trying to decide what she would say. There was one thing she would not say, she decided, and then she said it.

"I didn't know you liked older women."

"Drop it, Mercy," Cormack warned.

"Do you really want to be married to her and not to me? My mother and father would die."

"Your parents are dead, Mercer."

"I know her, of course. That is, I know who she is. She was at Radcliffe—oh, ten years before me. Well, eight, then. She is a large woman, isn't she?

Do you find her size reassuring? I can see that her maturity, her—her briskness, might be very appealing. Where did you meet her?"

"I am not thinking of marrying her for her briskness, Mercer."

"Oh, of course, not just that. Then there's her fortune, her title, her connections. Her four children. Isn't it four? Marrying her? Do the children come along with the deal?"

"I suppose so. I haven't thought about it."

"The house will be bustling. It's a good thing, I suppose, that she has so many children. You'll hardly miss Benjamin at all."

Cormack's eyes narrowed. "I don't intend to miss Benjamin. But we'll talk about that some other time."

Mercer went taut. This was it, then. The bottom line. "There's nothing to talk about," she told him. "Benjamin is my son."

"And mine."

"He is my son," Cormack repeated, and Mercer could see that he was now quite drunk. She had been longing a few minutes before to see some sign of emotion, to see tears in his eyes, and now she saw them. Yet after he began to speak, she realized he was moved not by any sense of loss but by his own words, by his own voice. Even the way his hair was falling into his face made him more pathetic in his own eyes. She watched him weep for himself as he reached for the warm champagne.

"He's my son, he has my name, he has my father's name and my father's father's name."

"Mine," she said quietly.

"Look, Mercy, you just have to accept it. Be reasonable."

"I think that I am through with being reasonable."

"At least go away for a while and think about it. Go up to Silvermine for a couple of weeks. I can arrange it. I have arranged it already."

"That place!" She was stunned. "The one where your mother always goes? Why should I go there?"

He was white with impatience. "As soon as I said I wanted a divorce, I could see your eyes light up. You've decided that saving this marriage will be your life's work, haven't you? It's the biggest challenge you've ever faced. I can see the busy little plans being laid."

"What would I do at Silvermine?"

"Rest! Talk with Dr. Schreiber. Swim, walk. Gain a little weight. Take some vitamins." He added, as an afterthought, "Maybe, when you get back, we can talk things out."

She stirred, rising to the bait. "Do you think it would help?" She tipped the champagne in her direction and shut one eye, sighting down into the bottle. "What did you tell them? You didn't tell them I was cracking up or anything ridiculous like that? They won't treat me like a patient, will they? I hope you didn't discuss your diagnosis with them."

Cormack took a deep breath and began to speak in his exaggerated long-suffering voice. "You are a stabilized paranoid personality, Mercer."

"It's not fair for you to label me like that!" she said. "You don't know anything about it. It's just meaningless jargon." Still she wondered. Was she a little more neurotic than she in fact believed herself to be? Was Cormack really just an ordinary, ambitious business executive, trying to arrange his private life to suit himself and ensure his own happiness? And did he have a right to do that? If she knew for certain which one of them was in the right and which one of them was in the wrong, things would be so much simpler. She realized that she had spent years passionately defending him from her own judgment.

"Look at you, Mercer." Cormack pointed his finger in her face. "You are oversensitive to everything that happens, and you are compulsive and overzealous in performing life's daily activities."

"What's wrong with that?"

"Defensiveness is another trait of paranoia."

"You could make a better case for agoraphobia. I am truly afraid of the World Trade Center."

"Humorlessness is another characteristic of paranoia," he stated.

"But that was both funny and true."

"Think about Silvermine, Mercer. James will drive you up. It is going to happen. I am quite sure, my mind is made up. It can be war, or you can hope to save something. Give it a try."

She looked down at the shambles they had made of the table. None of the food had been eaten, but almost all of it had been toyed with, disarranged, spilled. *Silvermine*, she thought. Would Cormack keep at her until she gave up and agreed? But she had given up, although Cormack didn't seem to know it yet. She felt on the edge of being ready to give in and go away. She needed to rest, she needed to stop worrying.

"Benjamin will be all right with Marie-Theresa," he said.

"Oh, I know. It's not that." Suddenly she was very tired. Perhaps it would be a good idea to get away, to make a break in the eternal bickering. She might gain a few pounds, lose the hollows under her eyes. A rest cure—wasn't it called that? Maybe he did mean for her to get calm, so that they could work things out. By the time she returned, the idea of marrying that woman would have blown over. The weather would have changed, and she would be like new. And, who knew? Once she gave up, things might change of themselves. Cor might begin to see what kind of marriage they could have if they were both really trying. When she came back, they could start over. They had started over before.

"Will you go?"

She would go away for a week, two weeks. It couldn't be any worse than summer camp, she thought. In fact, Silvermine would probably be a lot like summer camp. *I spent six summers in three different girls' camps*, she was remembering. *Camp teaches you something about operating. It doesn't do much for your head, but it does a hell of a lot about teaching you to be efficient, to pass your inspections and drills, and swim your two hundred strokes. Camps are very Prussian, very demanding.* "Silvermine," she said aloud, thinking what a short distance it was after all from no to yes.

She noticed that Cormack's chair was empty again. Where had he disappeared to? She heard a television set blaring from another room; applause and shouts, a reporter's droning voice.

She looked around the high, candle-lit room and at the slice of drawing room she could see through the double doors. Everywhere she looked she saw old things from Cormack's family, the few mementoes from hers. The dining table was one they had found in Vermont together. Cormack had said the proportions were perfect, and when they brought it to the city and put it in the dining room, it was perfect. "This is a lovely room," she said regretfully.

She walked around to the other side of the table. Cormack had left his champagne glass half-empty. The bottle of Scotch was completely empty. "Oh, I don't know, Mercer," she said in a mock-deep voice, draining Cormack's glass. "I'm a little tired of your taste. I'm a little tired of your menus, they're beginning to repeat. I'm a little tired of your bony hips. I can't even bear to be in one room and to hear you sigh in another."

Was that how Cormack felt?

The candidate that Cormack was not backing was winning the debate. Cormack could not find another bottle of Scotch. He had pulled a bottle of slivovitz from the back of the liquor cabinet and was carrying it around the apartment, stalking from room to room, half-undressed. *I'm glad I let the staff go tonight*, Mercer thought, before she remembered the real reason she had done so.

Cormack put the television set and the bottle on their bed, then came looking for her. As he walked into the dining room, Mercer could see that he was aroused. His eyes reflected points of light from the chandelier as he strode across the room. She grabbed the corners of the table and held fast. He came around behind her chair and pulled her up by the waist, prying her fingers from the edge of the table one by one.

He pulled her down the long hall to their bedroom. At the side of the bed, she locked her knees and refused to bend, but he put his knee in the small of her back and she went down. "No," she said between clenched teeth. "Stop it, stop it." But saying it loudly enough to be heard over the blare of the television sent her voice high and the strength drained out of it. "No, no," she said, yet it sounded like pleading. It was not a voice to command. Had she ever told anyone to do anything? she wondered, as she struggled beneath him. No, she had only won where her appeal had been felt, and lost where it had not. Cormack did not take his knee away from the center of her back until he had dragged her clothes off and held her ready.

He divided his attention between her and the television set, making savage fun of the candidate he didn't like, cursing the man's promises and mocking his accent. Mercer's fist struck out and rapped hard against the television screen. Finally he stopped. He threw himself across the bed and was still. Mercer turned slowly to lie on her back, her hair across her eyes. Cormack slept with his fists clenched. The face of the candidate filled the TV screen like a moon. Mercer's eyes opened once, and she stared at the other two faces, Cormack's and the candidate's. She was glad that it was really all over and that she would never again have to be a perfect wife, and she thought how funny they must look lying there, three heads on the pillows.

CHAPTER FOUR

"My mother-in-law used to come here," Mercer said politely to the man behind the desk as she dried her eyes.

"Oh?" He toyed with his pen and made a note in a file, giving her time to recover from the tears that accompanied her story. They had flowed so freely, she'd had to put a hand over her eyes like a sun shield.

"Yes. My husband's mother used to come here and bring all her paperwork, her correspondence, books she wanted to read. She said it was the only way she could get anything done. When she was here, no one could get in touch with her except through her secretary or her doctor. She would organize her social life for months to come, plan parties, choose menus, send out invitations." Mercer glanced down at the expanse of waxed floor between her and the desk, and with horror saw that her tears had accumulated into quite a puddle. She quickly turned her eyes upward. Dr. Schreiber had followed the direction of her gaze, but he could not see the pool of tears from where he sat.

"And do you feel that you are here for the same sort of thing?"

"Evidently not." She put out a foot and touched the edge of the wetness. The surface tension broke, and the puddle spread wider. It was like the drowning pool in *Alice in Wonderland*, growing larger. She looked up again. Dr. Schreiber was waiting with a frown of puzzlement, aware that she was not completely attentive to the conversation. "No, I'm supposed to be here to think about things, get myself together, rest, think about Cormack's point of view. Well, actually that does sound a bit like my mother-in-law's system, doesn't it?"

"I think you are facing a different situation, Mrs. McCormack. Let's be realistic. When you arrived, you were very angry with your husband. You accused him of violence. Oh, it's a natural thing, angry words and wounded feelings. I expect you feel that Cormack has not observed the proprieties of marriage, don't you?"

She stared at him and her eyes dried completely. "To say the least," she said with a short laugh. She had already described the last night with Cormack, she would not repeat it. The doctor had shrugged off the details. He continued to talk about Mercer and Cormack as if they were two people who had come to a natural end of things.

"You're not worried about money, are you?"

"No. Cormack's not mean about money. I don't expect that to be a problem. My father died recently, and he left me a little money. No, money is not on my mind."

"It's the sense of failure that is bothering you."

She sighed at the futility of talk. "For a long time, it was that. I couldn't see why we couldn't be happy. There seemed to be no reason for our marriage not to work. Now I see that Cormack doesn't want it to work, won't let it work. I don't want to regard that as my failure. I have made an effort, you know, an enormous effort."

She glanced down at the floor again, and finally the doctor gave in to curiosity and half-rose from his chair to lean over the desk and see what was distracting her. They both looked at the wet spot on the floor and then they looked at each other. He cleared his throat and began again.

"I'm sure you have made an effort. I'm sure you have done your very best. Let's go over some of your options again. You want to think about the future. You could go away for a while, travel. Have you ever wanted to be in Paris in the spring?" He smiled, as if he himself were tempted by Paris, but she was looking down again.

"Your husband said that you were interested in developing a career for yourself. Horticulture, I believe he said. He is willing to back you in any endeavors along those lines."

She did not respond.

"You could have the residence in the city to yourself for a while, to be near your friends."

"Those are my options? They are Cormack's, aren't they? Dictated by him?"

"You must try not to feel bitter, Mrs. McCormack. Negative feelings are counterproductive. I know you are angry with Cormack just now. I know how you feel."

She hitched her shoulders in a rejecting gesture. "What I want right now is to go back to the city."

"Yes, that can be arranged when you are feeling better and when we've talked everything out. How did you sleep last night? Did the medication work?"

"Right now," she insisted. "Being here is not helping me, I'm afraid. I feel cut off from my life, frantic. I have the strongest feeling that I should be at home. As a matter of fact, I'd like to leave after lunch."

"Well, now, Mrs. McCormack, you can't do that."

She had not heard this note in his voice before. "Why not?"

"You do remember our little talk when I met you at the reception desk when you arrived? I explained to you then that you were signing yourself in to a hospital, not a hotel. Our amenities, our spa routines, don't mean that this is not an institution, governed by the laws of the state."

"What are you trying to tell me?"

"Why, just that you can't be discharged until you and I both agree that you are well and calm and have thought things out."

Mercer sat in the chair without moving. The pool of tears had practically disappeared, she noticed. She found that she did feel calm, now that she saw what the situation really was and realized what she had to do.

"Let's go over my options again," she said in a businesslike voice.

* * *

The thoroughness with which someone had packed for Benjamin was the first thing that struck her. Even the three-wheeler that was kept in the basement was gone. Who had remembered that?

Mercer went from room to room, her high heels clicking on the parquet floor or silenced by the thick rugs, until she had seen everything there was to see. Benjamin was gone. None of his clothing or toys remained in the Fifth Avenue apartment.

After a while she noticed that Mrs. Donovan was following her around the south wing, holding something out to Mercer whenever she paused in her survey. "What?" she asked. "What is it?" Then she saw a tray containing a pot of tea, a cup and saucer, and a large creamy envelope. "Oh, I see." The tea must have been Mrs. Donovan's contribution. "Thank you," Mercer said. The woman left the tray on the library table and disappeared.

She sat down and opened the envelope. The documents were prefaced by a letter on heavy bond paper, topped by the engraved letterhead of Cor's law firm. The rest of the pages were standard legal forms.

She skimmed the papers. They were not difficult to comprehend. The two parties agreed to an amicable separation. The single issue of this marriage, Benjamin Ramsey McCormack, age five, would be in the custody of his father, who would place no impediment to the arrangement of visitation rights and pledged himself not to impair the child's love and regard for the noncustodial parent.

So this was why Cor had wanted her to go away.

She noticed a second, smaller envelope on the tray. It was unsealed. It would be nothing of any consequence then. Cor would never put anything on paper that he would mind Mercer showing to anyone else.

The note, in Cor's handwriting, was brief and civil. It contained the name of a friend of theirs, a young lawyer. "Or you may wish to engage a lawyer of your own choosing." A junior partner at Cor's firm had been assigned to answer any questions she might have on bills, property, personal possessions, and so forth. Cormack would pay all legal costs, of course. He would appreciate it if she would not try to see Benjamin right away, to "give him a chance to adjust." She should feel free to stay in the apartment temporarily; Cor would be in Connecticut, but she should speak to Wystan at the law firm rather than trying to reach him directly. That was the way things were done, Mercer realized. Lawyers spoke to lawyers, accountants to accountants.

He set me up, she thought. That's why he suggested a few weeks at Silvermine. Not so that I could get a rest, not so that I could think about our marriage, but to do this. To turn me into the noncustodial parent. "Everything I know about him, and much that I don't know about him, leads me to believe that it was inevitable for him to do what he has just done." Grace's incantation worked—it distanced the speaker from complicity with the other person. "Let's try not to take more responsibility than is reasonable," Grace had said.

Mercer's suitcase still sat in the foyer where she had dropped it. She did not bother to unpack. She hesitated only long enough to stuff some additional clothing and shoes into a Bloomingdale's shopping bag. As an afterthought, she spread her grandmother's patchwork quilt over her bed and piled some things in the middle—books, a box of crackers, a tin of pâté, the Queen Anne candlestick—and tied them in a bundle. Then she put it and her bag in the back of the Porsche and drove out of the city as fast as she could go.

Twenty minutes later she was retracing the route she'd traveled from Silvermine into the city, except that at Interchange 15, instead of taking the left turn to Silvermine, she turned right toward the discreet estates that dotted the greenbelt around Darien. She had driven the route hundreds of times. She and Cormack had always half-lived in the country, especially through the summers and on long holidays. The year when Benjamin was two they had stayed there almost permanently; it had seemed so much easier to have a baby in the country. Even now, Benjamin preferred the Connecticut house where he enjoyed the wide lawns, the swimming pool, and the overgrown woods, which his imagination populated with bears and foxes.

She slowed down for the entrance to the private road that led to the estate. She caught a glimpse of the house through the trees, a rambling Victorian structure that looked particularly warm and inviting today with the summer awnings already over the windows. She passed by the entrance to the driveway and continued on toward a stand of spruce that hid the outbuildings, which consisted of garages, an unused stable, and a gardener's cottage. Beside the cottage was a half-walled, half-fenced bit of overgrown garden. The year they had lived in the country full-time, she had made quite a respectable kitchen garden of it. At one end there was a bower lined with rustic log benches. She and Cor used to walk their dinner guests there, cocktails in hand, to inspect the vegetables and to see the tomatoes ripening on their staked vines. Then they would walk the guests back to the house, where the long table, gleaming with Cor's mother's silver, awaited them. Cor picked up an enthusiasm for the garden from her, and became a public champion of composting and ladybugs. Sometimes after dinner, when the ladies went upstairs to use the powder room and to have a look in the nursery, Cor would take the men for a walk right into the heart of the garden and instruct them in relieving themselves from side to side as they walked backward down the rows. Cor's Wall Street cronies loved the ceremony, loved describing it in the city the next day. It was not the first time she had noticed Cormack exploiting in public the same activities he called in private her eccentricities.

Mercer edged her Porsche between the garden and the cottage wall, tucked it out of sight, and walked through the woods toward the house. She could see the roof, an expanse of gray shingles that spanned the enormous attic, and as she came closer she caught a glimpse through the trees of the wide verandahs that surrounded the house on three sides.

She was almost tempted to keep going, to walk up the steps and through the door that led to the breakfast room and then to the pantry and kitchen. She hadn't eaten since breakfast, nor drunk anything but Mrs. Donovan's tea, and her throat was parched. She thought of the huge kitchen and its bank of refrigerators and freezers. With Cormack in residence, she'd be able to find anything at all. But she stayed where she was, watching the house, occasionally glancing at her watch, sometimes walking away from her vantage point to pace through the trees and work off the stiffness and fatigue that were settling upon her.

Cor's Chrysler was not in the driveway. He must be in the city today. That meant he would be back . . . around six, perhaps six-thirty. Benjamin would be given his dinner before then. Lights would begin to go on in the house. So far, she had not seen a single sign of life.

Just then the side door burst open and Benjamin ran out, followed by Marie-Theresa. Mercer jerked away from the tree trunk she was leaning against.

Benjamin carried a boat under each arm and clutched a third by the mast. He headed for the swimming pool, Marie-Theresa hurrying behind.

Mercer stepped through the trees and followed them, glancing warily at the house. No other figure appeared.

Benjamin knelt by the side of the pool and

launched his boats. Marie-Theresa hovered over him, warning him not to lean too far. *"Faitez attention, Benjamin!"* she said.

"Marie-Theresa," Mercer said, and the girl whirled around.

"C'est vous, madame!"

"I'm going to take Benjamin with me. It will be all right."

"Mommy!" Benjamin greeted her happily. "Look, a race. The blue boat is racing for you, and the red one for Daddy, and the big one for me." He stirred the water with his hand, urging the little ships onward.

"Madame, I lose my position."

"I know," said Mercer. "It can't be helped. Benjamin, we can't wait for the end of the race. I'm sure your boat will win. Come, sweetie. We're in a hurry. Mommy's car is just over by the garden. Come on now. We have to hurry."

He came with her without a question. At least Cormack hadn't told him anything frightening about her, she thought.

"Good-bye, Marie-Theresa. Thank you for taking care of him. I'm sorry about all this."

The girl watched them forlornly as they walked toward the trees. Then she turned and went into the house.

Mercer was sitting on the beach at Wellfleet when Cormack found them. She was sitting with her feet buried in a mound of sand, where she had obligingly left them so that Benjamin could mold a house around them. When he gave her the command, she would slide her feet out, leaving a neat small beach house for a shore crab to move into. Meanwhile, Benjamin had walked down to the tidemark to collect flat jingle shells to make a path to the shore crab's door. He had been gone a long while. Still Mercer sat with her feet in the sand. Her head, too, was covered. She wore a hooded pullover, with the hood up over her ears; only her legs were bare to the thin spring sunlight. Why did we come here? she was wondering. Perhaps it was the pull of childhood summers on the Cape, summers spent in maniacal training to perfect her riding, swimming, handling of a canoe.

She had gone to camp every summer from the age of nine onward. Camp was supposed to teach you to cope, she reflected, to be self-reliant. All it had done for her, though, was teach her to pass the next test, earn the next badge, jump the next hurdle. It was no different from the rest of life. And in an emergency, none of the readiness came back. Or did it? Hadn't her grandmother once said, "Mercer is beautifully equal to the emergency"? Mercer cherished the memory of the words, although she could not remember what she had done to merit such praise. Faced down a strange dog perhaps.

What would her grandmother think of her now? She had run away. She had definitely run away. She had not stayed to stand her ground, but had picked up her son and taken flight. She had hesitated only long enough to pack a shopping bag, to throw some useless items into the middle of her grandmother's quilt, and then she had driven out of the city as fast as she could go. "Stand up straight, Mercer," her grandmother would have said. "Stand up straight and look your problem right in the eye."

Mercer shielded her eyes against the sun's glare; she was beginning to have a headache. She had been facing her problem for a long time, she thought. More than a year. She had been looking her problem right in the eye for so long, it was a wonder she hadn't gone blind. Her marriage was a wreck. She hadn't even called a lawyer. Once she got out of Silvermine, she had not thought of any other solution but flight.

Maybe that was her mother's example. Her mother, too, had left a marriage, physically fleeing from it. But that was after she had drunk herself into absence, after many years of being only half-there. When Mercer was young, her mother had been fine. Competent and energetic. Mercer recalled the family verdict: "Just marvelous in a time of crisis, and never knowing what to do with her life when things were running smoothly." If Mercer had inherited that talent for managing a crisis, along with her father's day-to-day, hands-on-the-reins technique, she might have been anywhere but sitting on a deserted beach, shivering in the pale sunshine.

Her father's death had been a blow. How have I come through the last year? Mercer wondered. At least he hadn't had to witness her failure, the chaos of her life. He had been so pleased with the marriage, so full of pride at her wedding. She had surely fulfilled all his expectations—she had married into an old family, had married wealth and political power. When her father paid her bills at Radcliffe, that wedding day must have been exactly what he had in mind. He at least had felt that he had gotten his money's worth. Too bad it hadn't lasted a bit longer. Had she tried too hard, or had she not tried hard enough?

Mercer glanced up the beach. There were a few hardy souls in sight, but the season had not yet begun.

Down the beach, the haze shimmered and threw light into her eyes. Figures in the distance strolled above the breaking waves. Nearer, a man leaned over a child to see what he had in his pail. Sentimental tears stung her eyes. It was a sweet pose, it would make a corny photograph. The man's head was bent attentively, the child was absorbed in his treasures. It could almost have been her own family, if they had ever spent time together beachcombing. The boy crouched on the sand looked about Benjamin's age, the man paying attention could have been Cormack.

She slid on her prescription sunglasses. It was Benjamin. And Cormack. She momentarily froze, then relaxed. The shock was so short-lived, she was barely aware of the intensity of her response. She had already regained control, if indeed she was aware that she had lost it, and was already thinking of the next time. She sat quietly on the chilled sand as Cormack took the boy's hand and led him over to collect Mercer. *Next time*, she thought, *I'll take more money. I'll leave the car. I'll go to another country. I won't leave a single clue. Next time . . .*

"You are being very stupid about things," Cormack said mildly, ambling over to where she was sitting. He always assumed Benjamin wouldn't register the meaning of his words when he used that tone of voice.

"If I were clever, would things be different?"

"Things would be much more comfortable for you," he said. "Now, let's all go back to the city and I'll try to make you understand."

"Understand you?"

"That isn't necessary," he answered impatiently. "You are the one who requires understanding."

"Your way of understanding is to pin labels on me. Last time it was 'stress.' Before that it was 'nerves.' You told me you were in love with an actress, and then you went around telling everyone I was suffering from nerves. It's not fair."

"Come home with me now," Cormack said soothingly. "Come home with me and we'll sort it all out calmly."

Mercer went because she did not know what else to do. But as she trailed along the dune, stepping into Cor's firm footprints, she was thinking, *Next time. Next time I'll go . . .* Where? She had visions of deep woods, hidden lakes; of wide prairies stopping at the horizon. She thought of a little house, like a pale cave, where only her own footprints led in and out.

CHAPTER FIVE

Two weeks after Cor dropped her off at the New York apartment and drove back to Connecticut with Benjamin, Mercer was sprawled in comfort in Sarah's living room. The high windows behind them let in the white light from the city sky. The two women rested their heads on the cushioned tops of the overstuffed chairs and looked at each other lazily through half-closed eyes. Mercer was telling Sarah about her ill-fated odyssey to the Cape.

"I hope I haven't spoiled things as far as the court decision goes," she said. "I see now that it wasn't the smartest thing to do. It was all part of the idea to get out of Silvermine and just keep going."

"Courts usually decide for the mother," Sarah reassured her.

"I hate for Cor to win just because he's done things by the book. I should have been more patient."

"Nonsense. You were fighting for your child. The judge will see that. You're a fighter, better at it than Cormack. He has no imagination." Sarah shifted lower in her chair, resting on her backbone. "Let's talk dirt," she said seriously.

It was the signal for gossip. Only Mercer never called it gossip. Like Sarah, she had a theory about it. She thought it was the way women learned. By listening, a woman amassed a store of examples, statistics, case histories. All of the modern pollsters' methods had long ago been mastered by women. Like bytes fed into a computer, thousands of stories were recorded, thousands of theories tested, thousands of remedies spelled out, thousands of warnings remembered.

In the talk Mercer shared with the half-dozen women she knew well, every divorce was tracked and analyzed, from the first signs of broken faith and indifference through the rage and violence down to the intricate details of legal terms and divorce settlements. Other hours of talk were devoted to sex. And childbirth. The scraps of information provided by parents, teachers, doctors, and books, Mercer had decided, could never have seen women through.

She looked at Sarah across the old round battered marble table that held magazines, potted flowers, a silver pitcher of cold martinis, and an ancient Limoges soup plate for an ashtray, along with their propped-up feet, clad in Frye boots, like part of the table's eclectic collection. Mercer gazed at their long legs in their tight jeans and the comfortable aged creases in the boots.

"Sixties dressed up for the Seventies," she said.

"It was my all-time favorite decade," responded Sarah. "I just can't seem to let it go." She looked at Mercer over the rim of her glass. "You look thin."

"You look good."

"I'm okay. Actually, I just realized I haven't seen you for ages. I was away for a month, and when I came back you were up in Connecticut. I haven't seen you since your father died. How was the funeral?"

"Terrific." Mercer found herself saying that to everybody. "The funeral was terrific."

"Did Cormack go?"

"No, he wouldn't go. I went by myself. I preferred it that way. Cor didn't know any of Daddy's second family anyway."

"Hard on you."

"Not really. Although I find myself using it now for an excuse. Not to go out. Not to do anything."

"Does Cormack go out?"

"Cormack? Oh, yes. At least, that's what I hear. Cormack goes out."

"Then you must go out."

"Actually, I did. A few nights ago. I did go out."

"Did you really?"

"I went home in a taxi with a man who said 'Oh, well.'"

"Tell," commanded Sarah, slouching even lower in her chair. "Tell before the others get here, so I can hear it twice. Was it Alan?" she guessed, naming a West Coast filmmaker who had been showing up everywhere.

"No, not Alan. Nobody who was at Harriet's party. No, it's no one you know. I've been going out a little by myself, and it's funny. It's the first time since I was married. People say, come to dinner. And a dinner party is just right, it's just about all I can manage.

"Anyway, I was seated next to this man, and during dinner he turned to me and said, 'You know, I have the strongest feeling that you are about to bolt. Are you a bolter?' And I said no, no, you're completely mistaken about me. It shook me up a little, because I was feeling delighted to be there and quite strong about it, but we went on talking. And then after dinner some of us went dancing. None of us knowing each other very well, but just going on impulse. We went to that place, you know, in the bottom of that hotel in midtown. And later I came home in a taxi with this man I didn't even know. Except I knew that he had been married and had a couple of children, and I knew vaguely what sort of work he did. We'd had a very nice evening and the dinner had been excellent and we'd all gone out to dance, and he was dropping me off on his way home, which I thought was very nice. But then as we were going crosstown, he said, 'Well, now, what if we didn't go home? What if we just kept on going?' "

"My God, what did you do?"

"Oh, I had an anxiety attack. I said to myself, what am I going to do? Shall I? You know. And I couldn't remember what I used to say in those situations. So I told him, look, my father just died. I've just been separated from my husband. I guess I'm still pretty strung out. It's wonderful to be out, and all dressed up, and I appreciate the lift, I really do. But no.

"But, Sarah, here's the thing. I felt I could! I felt I could do it. But I thought, my God, I've got to think this over. I've got to understand what I'm doing.

"Because he wasn't hopeless. Not like Alan. Yes, Alan did ask me out at Harriet's party, but Alan is hopeless. Alan's the frog prince who is never, never, never going to . . . But this man in the taxi was not impossible."

"So why didn't you?" Sarah asked.

"Because while I was thinking all this, he settled back and closed his eyes and said, 'Oh well.' "

"That's a sad story. Sad," declared Sarah, who had stories that were far sadder. "Pour another," she said, and pushed the silver pitcher across the table with the toe of her boot. "What are you doing for money, by the way?"

"The usual. I've got a handful of credit cards, and the local tradespeople send their bills to Cormack's office. I have a little money my father gave me in an account under my own name. But I've never had any real money."

"Cormack's got tons. A bloody family fortune."

"He's never told me how much. He never tells me anything. I guess he's got a lot of money. Or his family has. Although something happened last year. They finally got around to the reading of his grandmother's will—you know, the legendary old lady who'd been living in Switzerland all those years. And he came home in a rage. He wouldn't tell me what it was about, but whatever she did with her estate—and it was in her that the real money in both sides of the family came together

—it didn't sit well with Cormack. We got some of her things—they came in wooden crates—but I don't know how the money was divided up."

"It's all going to come down to money in the end," Sarah warned her.

Mercer stirred uneasily. As long as she and Cormack had been happily married, her friends had regarded her with indulgence and pity. She was their innocent. Happiness had been her entrée into their group. Now, as the youngest of this set of friends, she was being initiated into rites the others had been through ahead of her.

She could not yet believe that the things happening to her were not singularly sordid but were—as the others assured her—mere detritus, and that she was passing through a time when there would be as much, and as little, to salvage as there had been of childhood and adolescence.

Now that Cor had smashed their life together, Mercer imagined that her friends were a little impatient with her, a little disappointed that another attempt at domestic happiness had proved so short-lived. Perhaps they needed one example of things working out to anchor them. Just imagine, Mercer thought, if all our lives were crashing at once. At least they had Ina, now, to inspire them. When Ina told them how happy she was with Sam, there was nothing they could do but rejoice for her. They were glad that the miracle had occurred before her illness was diagnosed as cancer, and then relieved to witness the further miracle—Sam, younger than any of them, pushing and pulling and bullying them all through Ina's surgery, forcing them to accept it at least as well as he did.

Almost as if reading her mind, Sarah asked, "Have you noticed the way Ina is looking more and more like the Dalai Lama? The same expression in the eyes, the same smooth fine skin, the same sweetness about the mouth. Oh, she's too thin, I think. Let's make her eat more, let's stuff her with deli from Zabar's."

"Where is she? And where's Grace?"

"They're coming, they're coming."

The four women had known each other a long time. Sarah had been the first to have an affair. They had all been at a benefit party for Lincoln Center when they watched an absolute stranger leading Sarah around by the hand, coming closer to them until they could hear what he was saying. "Hello, how do you do, my name is Martin, this is my lover, Sarah." Only the first of many bombshells, Grace remarked later.

And Grace had been the first to be put in a novel. It had been on the *Times'* bestseller list for nine weeks. It was written by a young midwesterner who could not actually have known all the public figures he crammed into his roman à clef. They had recognized Grace in the book however: They had recognized her underwear. Grace still wore the blinding white cotton underwear of childhood, the underwear rich girls wear right through their senior year at college. Grace's photograph of the author decorated the back of the book jacket, but that would not have been enough to identify her.

They would not have been sure without the lyrical description of the white cotton underwear from Altman's.

And Ina was the first of them to be ill, to be really truly ill.

Mercer felt that the friendship she shared with these women was a model relationship. It was a daily influence in her life. She spoke to Benjamin with unbinding love, almost the same tone in which she caught up the telephone and said "Sarah . . . Harriet . . . Hello, Grace." And she tried to use the same careful, reserved, and truly concerned tone with which she spoke to Ina when asking Cor, "What do you need? How can I help you? What do you want? What do you really want?"

All of this led her to the theory that it might be possible to love friends with passion and a husband with coolness. Yet like most theories, it worked only when everyone was standing still.

"I'll get it! Let me get it," Mercer said when the doorbell rang. She swung her boots off Sarah's marble table and hustled to the foyer to see whose impatient finger was pressing the buzzer.

"Yo, Grace," she greeted the woman in the doorway. "You look ravishing. Or would you prefer ravaged?"

"Ravaged has a nice sound. Havoc sounds better and better to me as I get older. I'm looking forward to being a menopausal tiger. How are you, Sarah?" she called over Mercer's shoulder.

"I'm rather hoping that getting old is like being

stoned," replied Sarah. "I'm mixing a fresh batch of martinis in your honor. Come get a glass and stop talking about the distant future."

"I shall wear that deep, deep shade of purple favored by Roman matrons."

"Knock it off, Grace. Pull up a chair. How's the divorce? On again? Off again?"

"It's off." Grace dragged up an enormous peacock chair, which framed her like visiting royalty. "I'm not surprised. I always thought I would stay married to Charles forever. For one thing, we both have hay fever, so we both suffer at the same time. We go to the same doctors, take the same medications. It's so convenient."

"Even a convenience as enormous as that sometimes counts for nothing," Sarah informed her dolefully.

"And even if it did," Mercer added, "you might still choose passion over convenience."

"Oh, passion," Grace scoffed. "Fuck passion." She took a sip from the glass that Sarah passed to her. "Ahhhh. How are you, anyway, Mercer?"

"The lawyers are working out a separation agreement. Cor says he wants custody. I'm contesting. We'll see what the judge says."

"How are things between you and Cor?" Grace asked. "Are you speaking? Can you talk to each other?"

Mercer recognized certain milestones in her own marriage by measuring them against those in the lives of her friends. "Cor and I . . . we are sort of at the same point you were when Charles and his girlfriend took up skydiving."

"Oh, yes." Grace nodded and leaned back with her drink.

The three of them sat remembering Grace's stories of those days when she drove the Land-rover around on back roads all over Dutchess County, trying to guess where the pickup point would be, looking up at the sky to see the two distant dark specks appear and fall and grow, wondering whether she really cared whether the parachutes opened or not. Now she knew what Mercer was going through.

Ina arrived, as gentle and stubborn as a magnet, Mercer thought. The three women made the latecomer comfortable, gave her a drink, then sat in their chairs turning toward her as one would turn toward an oracle. Her fine fair hair made her head a golden dandelion.

"How are you feeling?"

"Are you all right?"

"How . . . ?"

Ina confessed that she was not feeling very well. "There is some pain," she said. She had cracked a rib somehow. The rib cage was not as strong without the protective breast; surgery had weakened the flat longer bones.

"You know, it's not the first time I've cracked a rib," she reminded them.

"But, Ina," said Sarah, "you're supposed to be taking it easy. Don't do anything strenuous. What on earth were you doing to crack a rib?"

"I have no idea," Ina said. "The first time it happened, there was some pressure . . . there was a weight. This time I can't account for it. It just fractured."

Mercer took her drink and went into the bathroom to weep. "God bless Sam," she said, splashing water on her face. It was only because she herself had not lain under the burden of love for such a long time that she understood what weight had first broken Ina's rib.

CHAPTER SIX

The second time Mercer took Benjamin, she was a bit more clever, more resourceful. She made plans. She closed out her bank account, the one she had opened when her father's bequest came to her, and she carried the money in cash in her jeans pocket. She destroyed her credit cards, one by one, with her nail scissors. She left her car behind and picked up Benjamin at his school in Connecticut in a taxi she had hired at the Darien train station. A teacher, new or a substitute, who did not know Mercer, was on duty at the door of the kindergarten. Ben ran into Mercer's open arms, and it couldn't have been simpler. There was no doubt that Mercer was making things more difficult for Cormack on this attempt, because this time he had to hire agents—private detectives—to find her. Later, she thought it was Cormack's bad luck that the one who ran her to earth happened to be Gabriel Quinn, the one man in the world she needed to meet at that moment.

By the time they were apprehended, Mercer and Benjamin had been gone for three weeks, ever since the judge in Connecticut confirmed Cor's custody. They had settled into their new locality long enough to begin to learn the names of things, the names of the plants that grew behind the dunes, the names of the fish that were caught offshore, the names of the shells they found on the beach. Long enough to fall into a new rhythm of life together.

What alerted her? Later, she would not be able to say what it was that made her look around and then sprint after the car that passed her on the dusty road.

For no special reason, she had walked to the corner to buy *The New York Times*. The village was far out on Long Island, almost all the way to Montauk, flat fields on one side and pine woods on the other, so far out that they could have been anywhere. It wasn't that she wanted to read the news so much as she wanted to just go through the paper, a ritual page-turning. She left Benjamin sitting on the railed verandah of the rented cottage, visibly busy with his Lego set, building something that would tempt a rabbit to forsake the potato fields and move in right away. All of Benjamin's projects are so domestic, Mercer thought.

It was a small community, strung along the old Montauk Highway with plantations of pine approaching it on one side and potato fields growing right up to everyone's back doors on the other. The Long Island Railroad had a dusty station on a siding in the pines, but it operated only during the summer season. To come by train at this time of the year, one had to switch from the train to the bus two towns away. Mercer had thought of London, and she had caught the first train out of

Grand Central. She had wound up not really very far from the city, but she had been tired, so had Benjamin, and it was as far as she could go.

Two minutes to the little newsstand and grocery and two minutes back. But everything she did was taking a chance, she knew that. It was probably the low scratch of tires on gravel, the too-rapid acceleration that warned her. She dropped the *Times*, pages fanning out behind her like white flags of surrender, and ran.

She ran hopelessly, running like a wild animal over the dusty tarmac, her senses cut off. She could not hear the car ahead of her, nor her own rough breathing. She did not bother to measure distance but ran, just running, carrying a pain under her ribs.

Dimly she became aware that the car had slowed ahead of her. She was surprised when she suddenly caught up with it. She ran to the front door on the passenger side and opened it. He's as small as a bird, she thought. He's a baby, still, really. She got into the front seat and put her arms around Benjamin, pulling his head into her lap.

She glared at the man behind the wheel while she struggled to get her breath back. He was middle-aged, but with some bony, lank tentativeness that made him seem boyish—high bony forehead, thinning hair, wire-rimmed glasses. She thought she knew his face. She did know that particular face. He looked exactly like photographs of James Joyce.

"Why did you stop?" she asked, as he turned

the car toward the Long Island Expressway. "Why?"

"I saw you in the mirror," he began. Then he hesitated.

"And?"

"You were running . . . bent over. You were running as if you were doubled over with pain. And you kept running. I don't know . . ." His voice trailed off. "Are you all right?" he asked her in the way people ask when they really want to know. She realized that she had made a conquest, although she wasn't sure how. Something about her had touched him. Or something about the situation had set him up to be affected by the child, the speeding car, the woman running along the roadway and growing smaller in the rearview mirror. Somehow, running after Benjamin with her arms wrapped around herself as if her guts were spilling out, she had won this man to her side. But what good would it do her?

She looked out the window, thinking how dull and witless she had been to be caught again, feeling the steady revolution of the wheels shaking her body, bumping up through her backbone and tapping against her skull. She was still breathing hard.

"Take it easy," the man said.

She gave a harsh laugh. "You must be a good detective. Cor always buys the best."

He turned away.

"You found me, didn't you?" she insisted. "You must be good at finding people." She waited in a long silence for an answer.

"Why do you?" she asked at another point on the long drive back to the city.

"What?"

"Look for people who don't want to be found."

"Well . . . often they do. They do want to be found." He began to speak at last. "Sometimes while I'm tracing them, I start thinking of how they're waiting. Wondering where I am, why I don't hurry up and come."

"That's your own thing you're projecting. It's a form of anxiety. I am an expert on anxiety," she explained to him. "I know more about it than anyone you ever met." She looked at his hands on the wheel. "You are a private detective, aren't you? What's your name?"

"Gabriel Quinn."

"Quinn? Isn't that Irish?" She lapsed into silence. He looked Irish, with his blue eyes and ruddy face and thin cut of a mouth. He looked like a man on guard against being assaulted—by poetry, by alcohol, whatever. Uptight. She slid her arms under Benjamin and realized that he had fallen asleep with his head in her lap. She pressed her hands against the shallow bellows in his narrow chest.

"Have you ever done this before?" she asked the man.

"What do you mean?"

"Gone after a missing child."

"Oh. Yes. It's common now. Most missing-child cases land on the desk of a private investigator. The FBI will not even take a report on a child case.

They say they are not in the business of repossessing children. And the police are generally negative about missing-persons cases—any missing persons. You see, a private investigator can handle things the police can't. Geographically, he's less limited. The police are not going to look for anybody outside their own precinct. I can go anywhere. Also, a lot of cases come my way because the cops are not interested in an adult who willfully runs away or disappears.

"I look for a lot of people, too, who don't know they're missing," he added defensively. "Missing heirs, missing stockholders. If they knew they were missing, they wouldn't be. But what you've done . . . Technically it's a violation of custody, not a kidnapping per se. Not a federal case." He waited, but she said nothing.

"I've been in the business a long time. Fifteen years ago, I had one runaway wife to thirty runaway husbands. Now, I'd say, it's one to one. Women are leaving, walking away, they don't bother to explain why. Husbands suffer some trauma—they bolt, literally. They get overextended in some way and they can't recoup, can't get their balance back. They pack up and leave without saying a word to anybody. They're not easy to find."

"Are wives easier?"

"Wives want to be found."

"Don't husbands want to be found?"

"Yes. They want to be found too."

"And you find them."

"Yes. They stick to patterns, you see. First of all, they don't go far enough. They go a short distance, stick within a certain radius. If they don't take the car, they go by bus."

"I came by bus. The last part of the way."

"There, you see. No imagination. Most people are doing this for the first time and they don't know how. They don't put much thought into it. They make it easy for me. Personal checks. Traveler's checks. They charge things on their credit cards. Car registration is an easy check. They usually leave so fast, they haven't had time to get a new Social Security number, new driver's license, new health record."

"But . . . teenagers," she asked, curiously interested in this glimpse into his profession. "What about all the runaway teenagers? They don't own all those things. Teenagers must be a different case."

"Now, yes. It used to be that a New Jersey kid could run away and I'd find him—or her—on a particular stretch of beach in Hawaii where Jersey kids wound up. Next to a stretch of beach where the kids from Mineola wound up. It made life easier for me. It's harder now. The Moonies, for example. If a kid goes with the Moonies, it's a long-term search. They're a hard nut to crack. The Moonies are impenetrable."

"How," she asked casually, "does one really disappear? I mean, if one is really serious about it?" *At the very least, I can learn something this time*, she was thinking.

He glanced over at her. "You wipe out your entire history. You never get in touch with anyone from the past." He was silent for a while. "You really didn't want to get caught, did you?"

She didn't answer.

After a while he resumed, telling her all he knew about leaving one life and creating another.

When they drove up to the front of the Fifth Avenue apartment building, Cor was about to enter the lobby and had paused to exchange a few words with the doorman. For some reason he glanced back as Quinn's car pulled up. He spotted the boy. He saw her. He charged over to the curb. "No, no," she was saying, seeing it coming. He pulled Benjamin off her lap and out of the car, although her arms were still around him. The violence in the scene was perfectly captured by one of the paparazzi on permanent stakeout around their block to catch the resident Kennedys in the next-door building on their way to dinner or the theater. The man ran toward them, holding his camera to his face.

It was a good picture. Associated Press picked it up for syndication and it ran in newspapers around the country as well as in a few tabloids in Europe. Harriet sent a clip she'd seen in Morocco. The photo won a minor award, the Fairclough Prize for Photojournalism.

In the photograph, Mercer looked more or less the way she must have looked running after Quinn's car out at the end of Long Island: The open-mouthed calm of a long-distance runner. Benjamin, tousle-haired and big-eyed, looked fairly indifferent to the danger of being pulled apart between his parents. Oddly enough, Cormack was the only one who looked frightened.

CHAPTER SEVEN

Mercer always had the Fifth Avenue apartment to herself those days. She was there then and was beating her forehead lightly against the full-length mirror, hard enough to hurt but not hard enough to bruise.

The lawyers had cleared it for her to occupy the apartment for the next six months. She had lost almost everything else. After her second attempt to take Benjamin away, the separation agreement had been rewritten, curtailing her visitation rights. The Connecticut judge had seen things Cor's way.

She was standing in her dressing room, which was still steamy from her bath, trying to decide what to wear. What does one wear to a press conference? Your very own press conference, one that you've called yourself to embarrass your husband? Estranged husband, she amended. She had called Cormack at his office. "May I tell him who is calling?" a secretary had asked. "His estranged wife," Mercer had answered.

Grace told her to wear the blue outfit with the blazer jacket. "Don't wear any of your Zen boutique rags." A blazer is traditional, and faintly militaristic. A blazer makes a statement, Grace had said. "You want to look very serious and purposeful and maybe even a little matronly."

Sarah had said, "Wear the rose-colored Dior. It's your color and you look marvelous in it. They'll melt."

Mercer loved the ritual of dressing. In the past year, this had sometimes been the only occasion when she and Cor did the same thing at the same time, those moments when they were dressing to go out, sharing the big mirror, offering neutral advice on dress and style. She always tried not to fight before they went out, hoping for a successful, perhaps even a brilliant, evening.

She gazed at her face in the mirror. Would there be photographers at the press conference? *Probably*, she thought. *A photo opportunity. Why is it that I never think about the way I look? Unless someone reminds me, unless someone describes me to myself. I can't stand to be stared at. How do actors get past that horrible self-awareness? I can't stand to have my photo taken. It makes me feel self-conscious and silly. The only time I really liked my looks was when I was pregnant. A pumpkin. I was like a pumpkin, and I thought my belly was beautiful. Maybe I'm neurotic about my looks. But I think I'm only just now beginning to learn to live with what I look like.*

It had been hard on her when she was a teenager, growing up so fast in a few short months. She had heard her father and stepmother talking about her new adolescent presence.

"Well, we can't count on her developing into a beauty."

Mercer shook her hair out of the shower cap and began to brush it. *I didn't mean to eavesdrop,* she thought. *I never do that. I never read other people's mail. I just can't. I don't. I wasn't even snooping the time I found those terribly expensive ties, the geometric ones with the fancy labels. I knew immediately that Cormack had not bought them for himself. I was looking for something else, I forget what, and I found the ties. And I thought it was funny, since I didn't think he would ever really wear those ties, to cut them along the lines of their patterns and lay them carefully back in the box so that he couldn't tell. Just to see how long it would be before he picked them up and they fell apart. Cormack's lawyer made it sound so crazy in court. I thought it was a very funny thing to do with ties someone else had given one's husband. . . .*

"We've got to do something about her."

That particular day she had been walking through the hall of her father's house. The door to the library was open. Her father and stepmother were there. She overheard their conversation. Part of their conversation, she amended. And there was only one "she." Mercer knew immediately who they meant. Who else could they have been talking about?

"At least she could learn to move well, carry herself well. . . . There are places."

Not quite hopeless, it seemed. And so it was decided that she should be sent to charm school. No doubt the lessons she learned there would be useful today. "Gentlemen of the press, observe! Mercer McCormack is one of those people who can snatch up an umbrella or a pair of dark glasses and make an entrance: Glide, point, hand on hip, turn, glide, thump!"

She walked back and forth before the big mirror. Look at that, she said to herself. That carriage, that gait. Mercer, why are you scratching your crotch? Stop it immediately. Show some poise. Lift your chin. Not that much. Oh, the hell with it.

Yes, gentlemen, because I was considered unusually plain and with little hope of becoming anything much in the raving beauty department, it was decided that at the very least I would have good carriage. I was sent to charm school, where they promised to produce not a swan, but a girl who would make the most of what she had.

Every Saturday morning from the end of October to the end of December her stepmother had dropped her off at Magnin's. The department store had set aside a small private room half-filled with gilt wire chairs. She remembered an older woman with a modulated voice who conducted the class, an ex-model who was sort of depressed but still knew how to move, who would get up on the little stage and demonstrate her thighs or show them how to remove a fifteen-button glove.

The car let her off at the side door. There were a lot of other girls; the class was open to twenty students at a time. The other children were mostly fat. Mercer was thin. She had no hips, her legs started at her waist. She was called Twiggy, Daddy Longlegs, Starvin' Marvin. She didn't call names back.

We would go in together, Mercer remembered,

this pathetic group of children. Something was wrong with us, and charm school was going to set it right. We were going to gain self-confidence once we had acquired charm and poise. We were all going to be princesses. I think none of us had really thought much about our looks before we got there, but by being sent there—and when we were taking off our coats and talking we found we were all *sent*—we began to think something was really wrong.

We were about fourteen, between thirteen and fourteen, one or two of us were only twelve. We were given charts about colors so that we could figure out how to always wear dark skirts with light tops. One of the ladies would tell us how to disguise figure flaws. She'd get up and put her sweater inside her skirt and that would make her ass look fat; then she'd pull it out and down over her hips and that would make her look thinner. One day she confided to us that she sewed a dart in her bodice because one breast was higher and smaller than the other. We were horrified. No one had told us we might not grow symmetrically. We couldn't wait to rush home and examine our own budding chests.

But the funniest thing, the really and truly funniest thing of all, was that they taught us to pirouette the way models do on the ramp. Just imagine those hopeless little girls mincing along, turning, striking a pose, running back to get in line again.

The press conference.

Mercer walked toward the mirror and gazed into

her own eyes. You are digressing, Mercer, she told herself. You are distracting yourself from the subject you should be thinking about. But she knew there were ordeals she could meet only by being unprepared.

They had had one—was it one?—formal lesson in charm that year when she was thirteen. An exairline stewardess had taught it. And they had learned that charm consisted of doing whatever anybody wanted them to do. To be charming, be accommodating. That was charm. That was it. Mercer had raised her hand and asked, "What if somebody wants you to do something you really don't want to do?" And the answer had been, "Well, then, you should smile sweetly and charmingly and . . . do it." Never say no. That was it.

Will you be ready to tell your story to the reporters? Mercer asked herself.

It's the only story I know, she answered.

There was one session in charm school when they were taught how to get through a door. A lot of our lessons were like that. Just how to move physically through everyday life. For some people it can be quite difficult. How to sit on the diagonal to minimize your ass. How to place one foot behind the other, so that people won't notice what big feet you have. Oh, God, it was just so pathetic because we were all so ugly then, we were still wearing socks!

But all of us, anyway, all of those little girls knew one thing. And I have learned it over and over again. That if you scream, your voice just goes up and up and then it disappears. Self-control is the only answer. "Beginning now," the little girls were told, "you must learn to hold your stomach muscles flat. For the rest of your life."

But, you know, Mercer thought, *with all that concentration on self, I never had a very clear idea of what I looked like. Tall and thin, lank hair, braces on every tooth. I was brought up not to look in mirrors.*

"Mercer, what are you looking at? You're going to be vain. Watch out. It's what's inside that counts."

After Benjamin was born, Mercer had attended an exercise class at ballet school where the class worked out at the barre. The class learned—Mercer learned—to look at herself in the mirror. She looked now, holding herself erect.

I had never really, really looked and seen myself doing things in front of a mirror, she remembered. *I just never had. So now I can walk around the bathroom absolutely nude and think, well, it's me, isn't it? Okay, I can live with it. Not so bad. The face in the mirror. I can accept it. I accept myself, that one, there, in the mirror. With all the self-doubt and the self-loathing of those adolescent years, it all turned out okay. And even when I was young, it really wasn't so bad provided one had the defenses, and of course I guess I had the defenses.*

Thank God, she thought, she was almost dressed. She had thought she'd never be finished with it. She walked slowly toward the mirror.

"Here is the plaintiff appearing in her own proper person, with her attorney attending."

Her own proper person. That was the way she had been addressed at the first court hearing, when she had entered the Connecticut courtroom with the young lawyer who had been assigned to help her from the firm Cormack had recommended. He had not helped her at all. That had been the hearing when she had learned for the first time that she had no legal standing in the matter of custody—even simply being the mother of the child in question carried no weight—because of her stay at Silvermine. At the hearing she was told that from that day forward she was to see Benjamin at Cor's convenience, and with his agreement, and depending upon her own cooperation, which would be defined by Cormack. But when had Cor ever thought her cooperative?

From that moment, she had never intended to observe the legal agreement.

She went into her bedroom and sat down carefully on the side of the bed. She dialed Grace. "I'm wearing the blue," she said.

"Excellent. That's excellent, Mercer. Do you want me to come? Just to be there, in the background? I'd be glad to meet you there. It's at your lawyer's, right?"

"No, the coward. I think he's intimidated by Cor's law firm. No, the press conference is being held at my detective's office. Quinn used to belong to Cor, too, but now he is mine. My . . . factotum. My agent. He's better than a lawyer, because a lawyer will only talk about ironclad facts with precedence, while Quinn, when he doesn't know something for sure, will guess. Very useful."

"So you're all set," Grace said.

"Not really. No. I think it's going to be one of

those times when I won't know what I'm doing until it's finished and I see what I have done."

"I still say you should tell them he beat you."

"Oh, Grace. Well, he never did. Nobody ever hit me, except my father. And he only hit me once. For praising pop art. That was years ago. I think I had just met Andy Warhol, and I was saying that I thought his concepts were interesting. I said, 'I love pop art and I love the show at the Museum of Modern Art and I think a lot of that stuff is really terrific.' And Daddy said, 'Oh, no.' He said, 'You are absolutely wrong. None of that stuff has any lasting value at all. A child of six could do it.' And I said, 'Well, you've never seen it. How do you know?' *Pow!* Right in the face. 'You fool!' he said. The only time in my life he ever hit me. He must have been thinking of all those years of turning the pages in the *Encyclopedia of World Art* and trekking around museums with me. Anyway, I can't say Cor beat me. He's not a monster. Is he? All he wants is his own way, and really everybody wants that."

"He's hurting you, wrecking your life, taking your child. I think it's wrong to spoil another's life. It's as monstrous as most people get. Mercer, listen to me. When you're talking, stick to the point. Don't tell stories, don't get sidetracked. Dear, the first of your very short list of faults is that the things you think are specific illustrations of what you're talking about always turn out to be metaphors. Don't hand a reporter a metaphor."

"I know what you mean, Grace, really I do."

"And don't quote the words to popular songs

to explain a point. Not everybody looks for the meaning of life in rock and roll. Just tell them that your husband is a bastard, has played a dirty trick on you, and that you are appealing to the courts, to the press, and the . . . the . . . I don't know, public opinion, I guess. The very least you can do is make the appeals judge feel under scrutiny. It will go to that, won't it?"

"I don't know, Grace," Mercer answered indifferently.

"Are you setting it up to take Benjamin away again? No, no," she said quickly, "you don't have to tell me. He's with Cor now?"

"Yes. In Connecticut."

"What a rotten thing. We all marry the wrong man the first time. I think, I really think, that it's the third marriage that has a chance of working. Look at Harriet. Blissfully happy. The secret may be to just go ahead and get the first two marriages out of the way."

Mercer talked to Grace until she felt cheered up and assured that the thing would be a success. The reporters would come. They would. Cormack was almost rich enough to be a celebrity, and the kidnapping story had an element of sensationalism in it, although Cormack had managed to keep the details of that out of the papers. It was the notorious photograph, more than anything else, that would bring them, the one the freelance photographer had got when he ran up and snapped them. Cor and Mercer were caught at such an angle that it looked as if they were pulling Benjamin, small and white-faced and half-asleep, apart between them. It was the first newspaper picture in years that had not identified her as Mrs. Benjamin Cormack McCormack III. Instead, it was "Mercer McCormack, wife of prominent Wall Street figure, holds her son Benjamin, 5, as his father tries to forcibly remove the child from her arms."

Mercer dialed Sarah's number. "What if I give a press conference and nobody comes?" she asked.

"I'll come," Sarah said promptly. "Where is it?"

"No, you can't come. It's supposed to be impromptu. And I'm supposed to be a lone woman fighting injustice. It's going to be held in Gabriel Quinn's office, right after the court hearing. He's the private detective who found me this time, clever man. My attorney has advised me against talking to the press. My lawyer insists on being called my attorney, he thinks it's classier. He's against the whole thing. The plan is this: If there are any newsmen at the court hearing, no matter how the petition goes, I am to invite them, on the spur of the moment, to meet with me in my agent's office on Court Street in forty minutes. The forty minutes is to allow them to call in a press photographer or two if they like."

"I hope there's TV," Sarah said. "You'd look great on TV. Have you ever noticed that everybody who makes it on the tube has slightly bucked teeth? Cor's teeth are absolutely wrong for TV."

"I'll just tell them, in chronological order, what happened," Mercer rehearsed. "And then I'll sort of try to tell them what it's like to go from lawyer to husband to doctor to judge and back again around the circle, trying to get some kind of handle on things. Trying to get my life back, trying to get Benjamin. It's like—Do you think reporters will listen to this? It's like that game children play in the school yard when they snatch something away, your hat, your lunchbox, and toss it from player to player, over your head, behind your back, dangling it in front of you while you run from one to another, trying to grab it back. It's a mean game. It doesn't feel like a game at all. Did you ever play it? I always hated it. Oh, Sarah, I can't remember anymore why we got married, I can't even remember if there was a reason. I can't remember! Cor was tall. He wore beautiful tweed jackets and carried a pipe and pretended to smoke it. My mother said he had a wonderful nose, one that would look good on the children, whether it was a girl or a boy. Perhaps his mother was saying the same thing about me—'good genes.' We were just students. Why, Sarah, Cormack was an English major! I thought I was marrying an English major! That's what he was. Damn Harvard Business School."

"Calm down. Concentrate. Don't try to cover everything. If I really can't come, Mercer, come straight here afterward. I'll give you rum and hot tea. I'll look after you. Okay, sweetie?"

Mercer hung the receiver clumsily on the cradle. She looked down at her long, slender legs. While she was talking to Sarah, she had completely shredded her stockings with her nails. Oh, hell, she thought, no time to look for another pair. She'd go bare-legged then, so what? It was something only Cor would notice. She could hear him now.

"For God's sake, Mercer, don't you own a pair of stockings?"

Quinn's office was filled with reporters and cameramen who began questioning her as soon as she walked in, dressed in the conservative blue suit she had worn to the judge's chamber, and still carrying a stuffed Paddington bear under her arm. The bear was for Benjamin. She had bought it that morning at Bloomingdale's. Yes, she thought, I am becoming clever. This will look wonderful in the *Daily News*.

The voices died away and the questions began to come one at a time.

"Has your husband broken the law, Mrs. McCormack?"

"Absolutely. Yes. You see, my child should be here with me. My husband is keeping my child from me by force and subterfuge."

"Do you have legal custody of the child?"

"Yes. My son Benjamin is almost six years old." *I sound very calm*, Mercer was thinking. *I'm doing very well.*

"Isn't it true that your husband has been given prior custody?"

"But in another state. That is in the state of Connecticut, where my husband's family's property is located. I live in New York, and the New York courts have given me custody of my child."

"What was the decision in court today?"

"Today I simply petitioned the court to grant me permanent custody. It opens a court action to—to—define my . . ." Mercer's energy suddenly fled.

She could hardly make her way to the end of a sentence. "We'll know in about two weeks," she finished.

"Why not fight the Connecticut decision in the Connecticut courts?"

Gabriel Quinn interrupted the flow of questions and answers with some legal information, and Mercer used the respite to do the breathing exercises she had learned years ago in preparation for childbirth. The technique was useful for other occasions as well, she'd discovered. Quinn stood there, tall and stooped, looking like James Joyce. He peered at the newsmen through his old-fashioned wire-rimmed glasses while Mercer looked at him gratefully.

Those glasses are an affectation if I ever saw one, Mercer thought, smiling to herself, for she knew it had taken a great search to find a pair of glasses like those. He probably picked them up in some antique shop and had his prescription put in. It heartened her to see a touch of vanity in this austere man who in a moment's impulse on a dusty road had become her captor and rescuer all at once.

"I don't have to fill you in, gentlemen, on the complications that course would involve," Quinn was saying. "Judge Hughes decided that the case is merely a matter of conflicting laws in two different states. He is making a limited decision, and we intend to abide by the law of this state. I need not even mention the fact that whatever Cormack McCormack wants in the state of Connecticut, he can generally get."

Mercer drew a deep breath and began to speak. "Because of the influence he has in Connecticut, I have no chance in the Connecticut courts of ever getting my child. I asked you here today, in fact, to tell you how he has done it, so that you will know, and the public will know, and the courts will know, how he has done it. He has been utterly unfair. And I—I have reached the absolute end of being quiet."

"Did he—" The reporter who addressed her stopped and coughed. "Did he give you cause to fear for your personal safety?"

Mercer thought for a minute of the judge's questions at the hearing today. How delicately they had been framed!

"Did he abuse you?"

"Was he ugly?"

"Was he guilty of great angers?"

"Was he guilty of deep hostilities?"

"Yes," she said to the reporter. "He has made me fear for everything."

"Where is your son now, Mrs. McCormack? With your husband?"

"For the moment." *But I know where he is every minute*, she thought. *I know what time he gets out of school. I know what day he's late coming home because he has gym. He'll need a haircut in another week, I know where he goes for his haircut.* "But I'm hoping his father will abide by the New York court's decision and let him come home." She took a deep breath and waited for the next question.

"Some of the news reports at the time of the second kidnapping—abduction—mentioned that you had been under psychiatric treatment," said one of the reporters diplomatically. "Did that have anything to do with the Connecticut court's decision?"

"Yes, exactly. I'm glad you asked. Yes, I was at Silvermine for a short while. That's one of the things I wanted to get on record today.

"A short time ago I was very busy having a perfect marriage and being a perfect wife and mother and having a terribly pretty apartment in the city and a terribly nice house in the country, and not really looking far under the surface or thinking about what I really wanted to do with my life. And actually, I was terribly, terribly depressed. Then my husband asked me for a divorce. And I went on being calm. Instead of getting angry and blowing up, I just didn't. I waited and waited, and I waited too long and then I had a terrific blowup. It was our anniversary. My husband suggested that I go away for a while and compose myself. He suggested Silvermine. It seemed like a reasonable idea to me because it was a tradition in his family to do that—his mother used to go there before the holidays with her address books and calendar and do all her social arrangements. And his sister used to go up and sort of get herself organized and healthy and come back and run things beautifully. I had always thought of it as something between a rest home and a spa. So I said yes, and saw Dr. Schreiber, and I went up to Connecticut and signed myself in.

"It was while I was there that Cormack had the separation papers drawn up. Had everything worked out. Later everybody I went to for help marveled over the thoroughness with which everything had been taken care of.

"My 'voluntary stay in a psychiatric hospital' put me in a very bad position in court in the Connecticut proceedings. It was a dirty trick. With all his money and his attorneys, he had to do it that way." She stopped talking abruptly.

"Do you, Mrs. McCormack, face charges for abducting Benjamin?"

She looked uncertainly at Quinn; he nodded his head encouragingly.

"The first time I took him, I had a right to. The second time it was an abduction in response to his father abducting him, really. If I had been capable of being a lot cooler . . . Well, it seemed as if everything I needed or wanted was being taken away from me. And I wanted, I thought, a modest amount." She remembered, unbidden, the childhood game she had described to Sarah. Keepaway, they had called it. The only point of it was to snatch up a possession, something valued, and keep it out of the hands of its true owner.

She looked around at the faces of strangers. She knew she had to continue.

"When I came back from Silvermine, Cormack had cleared out. I was supposed to find a separate residence, I was given 'visiting privileges.' " She paused, as if to comment on the phrase, but the words failed to come to her. "My response then was just to take Benjamin away with me.

"The first time I took him, I just walked in and took him away.

"The second time, yes, it was more elaborate. I had rented a small bungalow at the shore, in a small town where people keep to themselves. I used a different name, I invented myself. And that time it seemed as if it would work.

"But Cormack hired very good detectives. Not tough guys, you know, but discreet and quiet. And imaginative. None of this ever got into the papers.

"It was never a matter of child support, alimony, equitable arrangements. It was a question of disrupting my life or his, of what he wanted or what I wanted. And Cormack always gets his way.

"If he wants something, he gets it. If he doesn't want something, then he doesn't have to have it any longer."

"What do you see as your next step, Mrs. McCormack? The child is presently in the state of Connecticut with his father, didn't you say?"

Mercer glanced at Quinn. This was the question they knew would be asked, and the only one he had drilled her on. She would wait until the New York judge handed down his decision before she tried again to collect Benjamin, she had promised Quinn that much. But she never allowed herself to say what she would do if the New York judge declined to disagree with his Connecticut peer.

"I will do nothing," she said carefully, "that violates the law of this state or the rights of my child." *There*, she thought, *I'm not saying that I am determined to have a life with my child, somehow, somewhere, no matter what.*

"When do you expect to see him again?" asked

the same reporter, as if he were reiterating the previous question.

"As soon as possible," replied Mercer, and once again her voice sounded strong and flat and matter-of-fact.

CHAPTER EIGHT

Mercer checked her face in the rearview mirror. No lipstick on her teeth. Hair combed. Bright, alert, eager. "I'd hire you in a minute," she told herself.

In the office building of the publishing company that had advertised a position in the local newspaper, Mercer was shown into a glassed-in cubicle almost filled by a large desk. Stacked newspapers and proof sheets covered half the desk. On her side, a brass bar spelled out a name: Henry David Finkelstein.

The man across the desk was as fat as an apple. A black leather belt marked an equator at his middle, with a perfect hemisphere above and below. Mercer guessed that he had recently become so fat, because his hands and wrists were those of a thinner man, and his face as yet showed none of the plumpness of his body. He told her that he had just been appointed to the post of managing editor, and she wondered whether he had turned his body into so much flesh in an effort to bulk out his personality and gain an authority—at the expense of agility—to match his new position.

The result was a formidable property, a home for his ambitions, a fortified hill for his head to pillow on. And he wasn't finished with it. Before him, on one side of the desk, spaced out across the polished walnut surface, was a little parade of food: Mallomars, Fig Newtons, Twinkies, peanut butter cups. Benjamin would have stared with open-eyed envy at such treats.

Mercer wondered if he used the sweets as a reward for work accomplished, awarding himself one candy bar after each specific task—and whether the end of her interview would be signaled by Mr. Finkelstein popping a Mallomar into his mouth. Or perhaps they represented limits he had set for himself; no more than one candy bar in each of the day's hours. What a drama of temptation, victory, defeat. It was a few minutes before she could concentrate on what he was saying.

"We put out a simple, readable tabloid newspaper here. It's phenomenally successful. Read by twenty million people every week. We don't really deal in 'news.' We specialize in human interest stories. The old man decides what is interesting to humans.

"He started this paper twenty years ago and still runs it according to his own formula, a precise mix of pop psych, indignant citizens, grotesque coincidences, miracle cures, photographs of animals and children, and the assurance that the worst things in the world are happening—but not to our readers. Because we also print how-to stories, giving six easy steps—ten easy steps if there's space—ten easy ways to prevent the worst thing in the world from happening to you." He shuffled through a stack of materials on his desk and held up a copy of the paper showing her a bold headline: HOW TO BE LUCKY.

"The old man is convinced that it is his mission in life to select and dramatize what's going on in the world for his readers. He feels that he knows what the average person wants in a newspaper—and it's not the Pentagon Papers.

"To preserve the purity of his vision, he moved the entire operation from the big city—New York—to the town of Briney Breezes, population eleven thousand and eighty-four, about ten years ago. He himself has not been out of the state since the big move.

"He has created an isolated one-man empire. It helped his purpose to take his staff away from the distractions of New York City—away from the theaters, nightclubs, social life, and competitors to whom his editors could flee if he abused them. I have heard that his original idea was actually to locate the editorial offices and living quarters for the staff on an island, one of those islands in the Intracoastal Waterway, a garrison from which his paper would reach every supermarket checkout stand in the country. It proved impractical."

The man paused. "If you take the job here, you'll have to suspend a sense of disbelief, as well as a certain independence of judgment. But at least you can live wherever you like."

The managing editor rambled on about work schedules and deadlines. She listened to his description of office operations while he twisted in his chair, swivelling his body around until he was

positioned with his elbow on the end of the desk.
There the hand hovered. Was the interview almost
over?

"Then the job you described to me over the telephone is still open?" she asked abruptly.

The raised hand interrupted its vigil to wave her
query away, while the lecture continued.

"From this little town, the old man sent out into
the world his team of reporters: Half-educated
British boys from Glasgow and Birmingham who
had started as newsboys at sixteen, and half-assed
small-town American journalism majors, all with
an itch to see the world and a yen to travel on an
expense account. Every one of them learned better
than to come back and give the old man anything
but the story he was assigned to get. Any other
story—including one suggested by firsthand information—was unacceptable.

"But after a while, even the old man's credulity
was strained. He found that he himself could
hardly believe the stories his reporters brought
back. Ordinary people were visiting the afterworld
and returning to describe their experiences. Various spacecraft were being spotted on back roads
from coast to coast." Finkelstein dug out a yellow-
ing paper. ADAM AND EVE WERE ASTRONAUTS, the
headline proclaimed.

"And medical science was coming up with
something new every week." He reached for another copy of the paper and turned it around so
that she could read the front page. SURGEONS CAN
CURE HEMORRHOIDS WITH AN ORDINARY RUBBER BAND.

"More favorites of mine," he continued, holding up an issue in each hand. FAMED PSYCHIC'S HEAD EXPLODES, she read on one side. DONOR SUES: GIVE ME BACK MY KIDNEY! the second headline proclaimed.

"The old man's next move was to create a fact-checking department, to check on the accuracy of the reporters and verify their stories. If you had turned up in those days, that's what you would be doing.

"However . . . as it turned out, all the stories were true, after all. Young men really do marry grandmothers, doctors do promise miraculous cures, and movie stars really fall head over heels in love week after week. It is all true, as true now as it ever was.

"Now the research department is simply a fact-checking operation. There's an opening there for someone who knows how to use the standard reference books, who can verify dates and the spelling of names, and keep the clip files organized. How does it sound?"

"Fine," she said. She had already told him, in their first conversation over the telephone, that she could do that. Anybody could do that.

"How do you like Florida?" he asked, sitting back and indicating that the formal part of the interview was over by snatching up a piece of food, so quickly that she had to look to see what was missing. Ah. The Fig Newton.

She thought about his question. She never knew what answer to give to that opening gambit. When Florida is nice, she thought, it's as nice as the womb. The air around you is the same temperature as the air you breathe; the sea is as warm as your bath. "I don't know yet. Do you like it?"

Of course he liked it. "Who wouldn't like it?" he demanded.

"I don't know, I feel sort of shipwrecked here," she admitted. "Sometimes I think I'm in the wrong place. Maybe I just haven't gotten used to it yet."

"One can develop a sense of place anywhere," Henry David Finkelstein told her, as if you could swallow it; as if it were a matter of eating enough oranges and grapefruit.

Still, he was not really mad about the place, she sensed. He won't be willing to outwait the patient Seminoles who have retreated into the swamps to see it through until we all give up and go. Or those other abiding ones, the young surfers, waiting out there in a line offshore like patient brown seals, bobbing on the waves, waiting for the day's big one to bring them in. Floating, one arm over the board, they've got plenty of time. The Indians and the teenagers are the only ones who really like it here. Let's all go back where we came from, she almost suggested to the unhappy editor, and let the young surfers and the ancient swamp dwellers fight it out over this particular strip of coast.

"Who wouldn't like it?" Henry David Finkelstein asked again, and she looked at him and saw that despite the efficient air-conditioning, the man was bathed in an inner sweat.

"I'll start tomorrow, then," she said, rising, relieved that the interview was over.

* * *

"Hi," Mercer called to her neighbor, who was waxing her car at the curb as Mercer pulled up in the driveway next to hers. Susan and Thomas Peale had been the first inhabitants in the row of town houses, and still seemed to feel responsible for setting the tone of the neighborhood and for initiating the modest amount of socializing that went on among the residents. Because Susan and Thomas spoke to everybody, relaying news and gossip, they all felt they spoke to one another. The Peales had already seen several couples come and go, opting for a detached house west of town when their growing families made the town houses too small. "They're fucking themselves right out of this neighborhood," Thomas grumbled. "They will never be able to afford to live on the water again."

Thomas, an airline pilot, was often away, and Susan cut the grass and tinkered with the car when he was gone. "I'm sure it will rain," Susan wailed to Mercer, "now that I've gone and waxed the car."

"Yes, I thought the weatherman hedged a bit this morning," Mercer replied.

How the weather forecasters hated to admit that it might rain. Afraid a tourist might overhear, she supposed. Everybody talked about the weather here. In New York the weather didn't count. The time, yes. In New York she had always known within a minute or two what time it was, without looking at a clock, but the weather had been a negligible factor.

"That's right," Susan said, "but he didn't say

'seasonal weather.' When he says 'seasonal weather,' then I know it's going to rain."

Mercer paused at her front door, checking the mailbox out of habit. There was nothing in it. She expected nothing; nobody knew her address. It would be nice to get some mail, though, she decided. She would subscribe to *The New Yorker, The New York Review of Books, Vogue*. Would they honor her subscriptions? Mercer, the deserter, the outlander. *Outlandish is exactly what I feel*, she thought.

In reaching this hard, white place, burning her bridges as she went, she had left it all behind. She had been clever this time. Not like the first time, when she had simply piled everything in the car and left. Everything, that time, meaning Benjamin, stuffed toys, clothes, her checkbook, some china mugs, the framed photographs from the drawing room, the Queen Anne candlestick, and as many books as she could tie in a blanket. They had registered at a motel on the Cape, and after a few days of sitting on the beach, Cor had found them. That was the time they all went back to the apartment in the city, and Cor was so civil to her that it was a wonder she didn't give in and do what he wanted her to do—give him a divorce—out of sheer gratitude for his gentleness and courtesy. Instead, she had been tempted again to try to save the marriage. Oh, Mercer, what a soap opera.

During this time, she had overheard him say to someone, "Yes, I like my wife in a bit of a hat, but back, off the brow," and was struck with amazement. At first she thought he had made up the woman he described and the relationship he implied, and then she decided that he was speaking of someone else entirely. She, Mercer, never wore a hat at all.

The first time she left had been a tryout, a run-through. This was not at all like that first time, she thought. Or even the second. This time it was definitely going to turn out differently. She had her name, her home, her child—and now she had a job. She had brought away with her all the cash she could get her hands on, but the secondhand car she bought in West Palm Beach had taken a large part of that. She told herself a dozen times a day, and marveled over it: "I've got to earn a living for me and Benjamin from now on." The very thought of it frightened her. She had never consciously decided on work, independence. Just as she had been married a long time before she felt married, she expected now to be free a long time before she felt free.

Looking back, she could retrace every step that had brought her here. But how different things looked in hindsight, how incidents in the past seemed almost eventless at the time, only to stand out like channel markers later.

There was a time, she remembered, when she knew things were wrong, and getting more wrong, and she went on acting as if life was really quite perfect when in fact she suspected it was really awful.

"I was not looking terribly far under the surface to see that I was really very unhappy, and I couldn't understand why I should be depressed," she said to her friend Grace. It was at that point that she went out and got herself on a committee. "Sometimes I can be very good," she told Grace, "at finding out what I want to do and then finding out how to do it." She knew a congressman who ran a committee, and she said to him, "I would like to be on your committee. I am interested, I will work, and I will show up at meetings and be responsible."

The committee was quite conservative and didn't accomplish much, but then a chance came along to take a course in the evaluation of urban problems. After that there was a spot on an advisory board that was planning a new community high school. "I asked if i could do it, and they said yes. And then I—who had never done anything except sell subscriptions to a socialist newspaper in college and work two weeks in a factory one summer on a dare and marry at twenty—I got out into the big wide world, made friends, accomplished things, gave talks on community relations, ran meetings, did all the things that one read about other people doing, and discovered a sort of competence which I never suspected I had. And I enjoyed it very much. . . ."

Although, she remembered, Cor began to say then, "I think we should have another child. One is not enough."

"Oh, no, no, no," she told him. "I don't think I want that much responsibility again right now. I'm just beginning to get a different kind of grip on my life."

"Let's have another child," he insisted. "We've got to have another child."

And what had he said later, after the night of the anniversary, after he had dragged her off to bed? When she had lied, testing him, and told him that there would be another child? "You keep it," he said. "You can have that one, I'll take Benjamin." There was no way she could continue to live with him. No way.

Of course you got the job, she told herself. She had been determined to get this one. It might even be interesting, looking things up in books, getting information for the reporters, giving them background facts, statistics, contacts. Like a reference desk librarian at a library, knowing which source to go to, filing newspapers and magazines away. Not terribly demanding. You didn't prepare for a career, Mercer, but you're competent enough to get a job. Of course you left Cormack, she continued, without a trace of surprise, in her continual seamless internal dialogue. Of course you did. What else could you do?

CHAPTER NINE

I could wear my linen skirt to the office tomorrow for my first day of work, Mercer was thinking, *and alternate it with the blue Liberty-print shirtdress*. When she got her first paycheck, perhaps she'd buy another skirt and a light jacket or unlined linen blazer. She could get by on that wardrobe for a while.

It was early afternoon, but she mixed herself a martini and took it out to the bamboo chair on the seawall. She held the first sip of vodka on the back of her tongue, too cold to swallow. This would be her last day of idling around the house, of drinking in the afternoon. She'd soon be too busy for such self-indulgence, too busy to daydream through the long, hot afternoons. Her new schedule would be full of activity, leaving at most only an hour or two at night to drag loneliness and fear around behind her like a too-long dressing gown flapping at her heels. An hour or two was a manageable amount of time, surely. It would be a mark of progress to reduce loneliness from several hours of the day to two. If only she had someone to talk to.

What would be the harm of ringing Grace?

She had always loved talking to Grace. "Now Grace, listen," she would say. And Grace would draw in her breath and wait. Grace always breathed with the story—rhythmic murmurs, gasps, indrawn breath—eyes going wide, head nodding yes, yes. And she told her own stories with a dry irony and sweet twisted mouth.

Of all her friends, it had been Grace who guessed that something was about to break. Before Mercer's second, still amateurish attempt to take Benjamin and leave, Grace had asked, "You're cutting out, aren't you, Mercer?"

"No, no. I haven't got the energy."

"You've got it. You've got the energy. You could pull it off. You are actually very brave, Mercer. A pioneer woman."

"Brave!"

"I think so. I see you as a fighter."

"Me? But I'm against violence. Absolutely against it. I mean, what were the Sixties about, Grace? If we learned anything, it was that there are ways of being strong without being violent." She was quiet for a moment. "Do you mean that you think I'm capable of violence?"

"Oh, sure."

Mercer thought about it. "I do think I would know how to save my own life, if I had to. I mean, I've thought about what I would do if I got mugged, or if I were taken hostage in a bank holdup. That sort of thing."

"That efficient father of yours—didn't he teach you and your half brothers the manly art of self-defense?"

"Yes. . . . Sometimes I wonder if I wouldn't actually handle things better if I had not been the child of an efficiency expert. Such a strange standard. Efficiency."

The only people in her father's personal life he ever tried to shape were her mother and herself. And when he failed with his wife, he turned the full heat of his idea of female perfection on her, she told Grace. "Since my mother was so stubborn, I was supposed to become the perfect woman. I would be the perfect manager, the perfect cook, the perfect companion, the perfect . . . I was to marry well." She was taken to restaurants to learn the taste of different kinds of food and how to order it and how to talk about it.

Grace had laughed. "You, who go into garlic shock? Who thinks buttered bread with wine is a meal? Look at you now."

"I was even taken to a diner to learn how to manage a kitchen efficiently from watching the short-order cook. And, typical of my father, when we moved to our big house, he made my mother take a course in first aid before he let her begin to give big dinner parties. He was absolutely convinced that someday a guest would choke on filet mignon at his table. 'Everyone should be able to perform a simple tracheotomy,' he always said."

"You have to admit, Mercer, he prepared you for life as well as he could."

"Oh, he prepared me—to be a perfect wife. And I was a perfect wife. And that's why I'm in this fix."

But I got out, she thought now, fishing the melt-

ing ice cubes from her drink and tossing them into
the canal. She looked around at the comfortable
old wicker chairs she had found at Goodwill.
Home, child, job. A few domestic odds and ends.
This time, like the other times, she had brought
away a handful of things. Her favorite framed photographs: Benjamin in a sandbox in the playground in Central Park; Benjamin sitting in the
big blue Queen Anne chair in the New York apartment, holding his bubble gum ball out in front of
him so that the camera magnified it, making it look
as big as his head. People seeing the photograph
always asked what Benjamin was holding. Not
quite round, not quite buoyant, it was hard to
guess what the object might be. A terrible mistake,
she thought, not to have remembered to bring it.
Benjamin had saved all the bubble gum he had
ever chewed. It was in one enormous ball.

"It's like a religious relic," Mercer had once explained to a guest who asked about the photograph. "Benjamin can look at it, and it's his whole
life, in mystic layers, like pink petals pressed together. No, no, it's still pink—he keeps it in a
plastic bag. Sometimes he takes it out and passes
it around among his friends. They're quite awed
by it, quite moved to be allowed to hold it and
think about time wrapped up in this way." When
she took him away, she forgot to take the bubble
gum ball along. She shook her head. They went
off and left his past, sitting there on his night shelf.

And she had left her friends. She missed her
friends. Really missed them. "What I'd like right

now is to sit down with this martini in one hand and the telephone in the other and talk to Sarah."

Sarah had always defended their idle hours. "It's just our way of guessing about each other." Sarah's definition of gossip. Sarah said that Virginia Woolf thought so too. "Talk is the only way we have of knowing each other," Sarah had quoted.

Mercer turned on the radio. Funny how some commercials assumed the status of real songs. A rich contralto was singing suggestively about a local soft drink product Benjamin had warned her away from. "Have a Pibbs, Mis-tuh! Have a Mr. Pibbs! Mis-tuh!" The musical appeal worked in a funny way; it created the image of a Depression-style middle-aged man in a gray topcoat with enough money in his pocket to go into a diner and demand service. She could see him in her imagination—he looked like Charles Bronson. With such a persona, one could seem quite circumspect, and hide some wildness and readiness under a gray cloth coat. They could be comrades, the two of them, if they ever met in their gray coats. They would spend all the change in their pockets and sit together and drink Mr. Pibbs. They would tilt their heads back at the same time, like mourning doves at the puddles after a rain. His neck would look rather like a water hyacinth stalk. Trusting her, Charles Bronson would allow her to reach out and lay her hand across his throat.

It's funny, she thought, *no matter how angry I have been with Cor, with men in general, I can't think of touching a man's throat without feeling something,*

without feeling moved. It's so odd, that lump. The flesh
is so thin there, and something is pressing forward, as
if antlers are about to sprout. It's as awkward as a
naked soul erupting. My soul is discreetly attached to
an ovary, the one on the left. In a little pouch, big
enough to hold a penny—deep, deep, you'll never find
it. But yours, Mr. Bronson, is thumping against my
hand.

The longing to talk to someone—Sarah, Ina,
Grace—persisted through the afternoon. Benjamin came home from school with tales of snapping
turtles on the sidewalk. They went to look, but it
was too late, the snapping turtles had disappeared
into the little stretch of mangrove swamp on the
other side of the road. Mercer and Benjamin went
home to build a small fire in the hibachi for cooking Johntie's fish. Mercer had put it to marinate
in lime juice, and when the evening had cooled
off, they cooked it over the coals, basting it with
garlic butter.

After dinner, she was glad of a diversion when
Johntie and two of his mates from the drift boat,
Sasha and Tom, came over to sit on the seawall
and demonstrate for Benjamin's edification how
to throw a net.

The first time she watched the net go out, she
saw only the result—the lacy pinwheel falling
through the air. Watching again, she saw the many
exact steps that made it work. With the fishnet
over his shoulder, Johntie looked like a Mediter-
ranean fisherman. In his belt he wore a riveted
fishing knife with a scored blade, exactly like a

thirteenth-century dagger Mercer remembered seeing in the British Museum.

Johntie put a loop of the net's rope around his left wrist. Taking seven or eight hitches, he coiled the length of rope across his palm.

Next, he took the brass ring at the center of the net and held it high in his fingers so that the net swung like a skirt, the silver-colored lead sinkers flashing like sequins. He held one length of the net in his strong white teeth.

The last step was to flip a fan of net around his left shoulder and let it slither down his arm into his hand. He stood poised, leaning over the canal, his eyes searching the water. Mercer shivered with anticipation. Benjamin whispered, "Let go!" at the exact moment of action, without knowing he had spoken aloud. She loved the evening at that moment, and thought that it was as good as many social evenings she had spent in the city—better than most.

Johntie's toss carried the net out over the canal, sending it flat into the air, like a pancake, lifting up and spinning out from his hand, teeth, shoulder, hand, with the edge that had been held in his teeth raising slightly, like a lip, to catch the air. It filled and parachuted slowly down, the sinkers touching the water like heavy raindrops, plink. The nylon cord turned almost clear as soon as it was wet, and fell perfectly through the water, so gently that the mullet, which had darted wildly when the sinkers hit the surface, were lulled, and waited to see what would happen next, while the invisible filaments dropped around them.

Johntie let Benjamin haul in the net. It had a single mullet in it, whipping its tail from side to side. Sasha was allowed to cast the net next, carefully following Johntie's example. "Some more live bait, we'll catch a sailfish tomorrow," said Tom, Johntie's friend from the west of town. Boys from the west of town were rednecks and had a reputation for being simple and tough. The best way to be, Mercer thought.

She roused herself to be more sociable to them. She brought wineglasses and a bottle she had opened earlier to the bamboo table on the seawall. "Would you like a glass of wine?" she asked them. One of the boys, pleased but shy, accepted a glass and drank half of it off, quickly. "Help!" he said. "My ears are filling up with wine!"

The others laughed and slapped his back. Then they invited Mercer to put her wine away and share with them what they had. On the table they carefully unwrapped from a thin creased piece of tissue paper a Tai stick, a dried wispy branch threaded on a sliver of bamboo, crisscrossed with a peeled leaf vein as fine as a silk thread. "The best," Johntie breathed.

She enjoyed the ritual of smoking, and sat with them in companionable silence, passing the joint, once Johntie had rolled it and started it around.

It was powerful, she thought, after it had circled past her twice. It worked the charm that dope always did; it allowed people to be alone together. She hardly noticed when it was finished and the three young fishermen said good night and took their net and the mullet that would be their live bait for the morning boat and left.

She sat gazing up the canal, at the pattern of choppy waves on the surface of the water, the wild grass bending away from her, the willows farther up the canal turning their leaves in shimmering flashes. It looked like every landscape painting she'd ever seen. It was well-composed; you could simply put a frame around it and hang it. She missed the museums of New York, she really did; she missed being able to walk down to Eighty-fourth Street and see the French Impressionists; she missed knowing that farther downtown on Fifty-third Street Monet's water lilies had a whole room to themselves.

She sat on the seawall, still feeling a little of the sun's heat captured in the concrete, warming her thighs. She turned and looked down the canal.

Eerie, how in that direction the scene looked completely wrong. She had never seen this effect in a painting. Here, too, the pattern of waves disturbed the water, but instead of forming a design, it was chaotic. Even the light fell wrong, striking the back of the waves. And the grass blowing toward her, the flickering leaves, looked absolutely unnatural. What made the difference? she wondered. She tried to recall landscape paintings she had seen. Was it possible that every painter worked with the wind behind him? Did every painter prefer the leeward view? And did her view up the canal look more aesthetically pleasing because it was more familiar, conditioned by art, or was there an inherent quality to the view with the wind leaving you, leading you, in effect, deeper into the painting—not pushing you out?

Maybe I've discovered some underlying law of perspective, she thought. She danced along the seawall, her head feeding her more ideas. *If only I were an art history major, looking for a thesis*, she mused. *Or if I had somebody to talk to*. The idea was too wordy to try to get it across to Johntie, with her limited vocabulary of sign language, and too complicated for Benjamin. Hadn't Sarah been an art history major? *If only I could talk to Sarah.*

Mercer sat beside the water for another hour while Benjamin made himself a peanut butter sandwich and did his homework. Just before she roused herself to go inside, still a little light-headed from the Tai stick—the wind was beginning to die down and the tiny biting insects her neighbors called no-see-ums were descending on the banks of the canal—she looked one more time at the patterns of light and wind on the canal. It occurred to her that there was a perfectly practical, mundane reason why those artists who left their studios in the nineteenth century and ventured out into the countryside to paint from nature made it a habit to set up their easels and paints so as not to face into the wind. Canvas and paint would have come blowing into their faces. Of course they set up their paraphernalia with the wind at their backs—only a fool would do differently.

How strange the world was. Throwing a net seemed to be one simple step, yet it was not. Choosing a perspective seemed to be a matter of some complexity, but a brisk wind could simplify it greatly. You couldn't tell by the surface of an act what preparation went into it. Although Mercer generally accepted the act as the outward manifestation of inner complexities, she thought that people did what they did simply because they had to. They perceived themselves as having no other choice. Everybody does what he had to do, she insisted. "I did what I had to do." People do what they do—from loving to painting to stealing a child—because they have to do it.

But if that's so, she asked herself, what about Cor? Because Cor had acted from something colder than necessity. When he sent her to Silvermine, he had set a trap for her and deliberately led her into it.

Wow, she was zonked. Coffee with a lot of sugar in it would bring her down, she knew, but instead of reaching for a cup and saucer, she reached for the telephone. Without thinking she found herself dialing a familiar number.

There would be no way to trace the call. And even if word did get back to Cor—well, Cor knew after all that she wasn't dead. That she was somewhere, reading, sleeping, drinking too much coffee, making her famous soufflé, wearing her same old scarlet silk dressing gown.

"Sarah!" Mercer felt tears start in her eyes. She was grateful that her call had been answered.

"Mercer! Hold on—I'll be with you in a moment."

Mercer clung to the telephone, wondering if she had done anything irreparable, and wondering

what Sarah was doing—wrapping her hair in a
towel? Shooing a lover out the door?

"So, where are you?"

"Sarah, you sound so—so good. Never mind
where I am. Have you . . . have you seen Cormack?"

"Yes. Yes, I have. He's cut his hair."

Mercer snorted with laughter and wiped her
nose. Oh, Sarah, she thought gratefully, tell me
more.

CHAPTER TEN

Why was this morning so bad? Mercer wondered. *And why this particular morning?* She thought she had the morning routine licked now that she had been working for a few weeks, but she had awakened full of anxiety, the wrong song warming up the clock radio. Something disastrous was going to happen. Or was it just that the barometer was falling? When a weather front moves in and the barometer starts to fall, Johntie had told her, the fish go crazy. He had demonstrated, turning his forearms into the lowering atmospheric pressure, pushing his flattened hands downward, slapping at an invisible line that marked the surface of the sea; then he had wagged his head like a dopey fish, swimming around the seawall in more and more eccentric circles. She could be suffering from barometric pressure, Mercer thought, staring at herself in the bathroom mirror.

She tied her hair back and pulled on a pair of jeans and drove Benjamin to school, hurrying back to wash the breakfast dishes and get dressed for the office. Just before she left the house, as she locked the glass doors that led to the terrace, she noticed the sea anemone in Benjamin's fish tank.

It seemed to be dying, waving withered mauve tendrils at her through the heavy glass. Johntie, who knew all about sea life, had assured them that such transformations were quite natural, that the anemone went through stages of expansion and retraction, that it could even draw itself into a scallop-sized lump for days at a time. But she had never seen it as shriveled as it appeared this morning.

Looking around for other atrocities—now that she expected them—she noticed that the little finch in the cage had a bit of something that looked like dried blood on its beak. She had no idea what to do for the bird, or even how to examine it for other signs of ill health. She would have to wait to deal with it until she came home in the evening. Perhaps the bird would manage to recover or die in the meantime, and remove itself from her list of anxieties.

Backing out of the driveway and turning toward Federal Highway, Mercer found the road in front of her blocked by a huge fallen palm frond, dried and hard as a rake, almost the size of her car.

"I have got to get to work!" She ground the words between her teeth.

"Sorry I'm late," she rehearsed aloud as she put the car into reverse. "My way this morning was barred by a palm frond." She turned the car around and left by the lane, going the long way around to the highway. She was beginning to believe that the day was lost before it had fairly begun; she was ready for anything now. "Stonewall it," she kept saying to herself. "You can get through this day if you just stonewall everything that happens."

When she slowed for the turn onto the access road to I-95 and saw a mangled furry shape on the raised divider on her left, she almost turned back. "I want to go home!" She moaned. There was a full-grown raccoon lying on the graveled surface of the divider, obviously dying, maybe already dead. She couldn't tell. It raised its head as she braked and she looked for a long moment into its eyes. It horrified her at first but then it cheered her up. She saw that when the universe contracts to the point of being filled with a single agony, it can be endured with something that almost looks like passion. She gazed as long as she could into the animal's eyes, then gave her attention back to the road, feeling a calm that sustained her through the morning.

A reporter stuck his head around the open door of the research department and leered at Mercer. "I hear you give great research," he said. She remembered his first name: Malcolm, a Scot transplanted from Glasgow to write sly gossip for the paper. He was hairy and skinny, and wore tight trousers topped by brightly patterned nylon shirts, always unbuttoned almost to the waist.

"Oh, look," she said with mock concern, "you've lost a button."

He rolled his eyes to show that he did not like her little joke. He only liked it when he did the teasing. But she was not in a mood for banter today. "What do you want?" she asked shortly.

"Where is Liza this week? Is her divorce final? Will she give me an interview?"

Mercer flipped through her Rolodex. "Here's her agent. Set it up through him. Good luck."

"Hey, wait a minute. I've got another question."

"Make out a query form and drop it in the box," she told him. "I'll do it when I can get to it."

"Oh, we're in a mood this morning. We haven't had our coffee yet," he said, coming all the way in from the hall and perching on a corner of her desk.

"What is your problem?" she asked, but he was absorbed with pawing his way through the stack of query slips in the box, hoping to see what information other reporters were after and to pick up something he could use in one way or another. The editors and reporters were extremely secretive about their story leads, and were guarded with their contacts and unlisted phone numbers. They did, however, market to each other on a cash basis valuable telephone numbers, celebrity contacts, and those story leads they didn't care to work themselves. Mercer was staggered by the amount of money that changed hands each week, over and above their paychecks. She watched Malcolm sift through the notes, thinking what a bleak morning it had been, bleak and hot, a combination that turned everything gray and drained her of energy.

She had complained that morning as she fixed Benjamin's breakfast, "It's hot, hot," swearing in the next breath that she would not turn on the air-conditioning until the calendar warranted it, saying that she preferred the weight of the heat to the alternative—dashing from one air-conditioned place to another. "Who wants to live in a wind tunnel?" she asked Benjamin.

Why had she headed south, anyway? She could not remember. Oh, yes. She had found an old forty-five in an open bin at a street fair in the city. Staying alone in the New York apartment those last empty days, before she plucked Benjamin out of school, she had played one side over and over. "I'm going where the sun keeps shining. . . ." Following the coast, she had gone almost as far as she could without winding up in the cul-de-sac of the Keys. She wondered if any of Cor's new detectives would be clever enough to play her records for clues to her whereabouts, her state of mind. "Goin' where the weather suits my clothes . . ." Even Cor, who had barely tolerated her addiction to rock music, could read her that way.

"Am I the only person who still buys forty-fives?" Mercer wondered aloud to the reporter, whose navel she could almost see as he leaned over the desk. "I must be supporting an entire industry." Malcolm kept pawing through her box of query slips.

"Go a long way," Quinn had told her. It had been autumn in New York, the air just beginning to turn cool. She had headed south. And she had kept going.

Malcolm lit a cigarette and looked around.

"What is it you want now?" she asked him. "Ash-tray?"

"Give me a blank query slip, will you, love? I've got another little job for you. I want to get hold of Amy Carter's high school report card. Can you get it for me?"

"Oh, Malcolm, really. Anyway, I'm tied up all morning. I have to get the Nielsen ratings on the week's shows, so Henry David can decide who's in and who's out. I'll assign your request to a stringer, but I can't promise anything."

"Who's the Washington stringer these days? Is it still what's-his-name, the reporter who went through Kissinger's garbage?"

"Uh-huh."

"Let me know how he makes out, will you?"

Mercer sighed and began to pound out a list of figures on the typewriter, telephone receiver crooked on her shoulder as she listened. She attacked the typewriter with a system she had learned from a self-help manual entitled, "Your B.A. Is Not Enough: Learn to Type in Twenty-four Hours." She typed well enough for the notes and reports she had to do here. One of her chores was posting the weekly ratings from A.C. Nielsen. Like most jobs on newspapers, this one was both vital and menial. Sometimes she wished she had more feeling for her work—more of a sense of involvement, more of a sense of commitment.

Wasn't there something to be said for answering a query quickly and accurately? Perhaps. If that were all there was to it. But usually a query came from an editor who was not searching for information, but seeking to bolster a story he already had in the works. If the answer she supplied did not support his story lead, then it was no good to the disappointed editor, who gazed at her with slack face as she cited the source of her information. Already this morning she had taken a query slip with its answer down to the editorial room.

"Professor Smythe, who wrote the article on this subject for the *Encyclopedia Britannica*, and the head of the state agricultural college, and the chief chemist at Du Pont, all say no, nobody makes dynamite out of peanut shells."

"Whaaat?" came the enraged response. "Who are they? What do they know? Ask somebody else!"

Although she could not feel much interest or commitment as far as her work was concerned, the job had begun to dominate her life. It took most of her time and a disproportionate amount of her attention. There were some peculiarities of the job that particularly sapped her energy. For example, anyone who was paid more than she was, which meant almost everyone on the editorial staff, was allowed to abuse her. She sensed she would be allowed to abuse anyone whose salary was less than her own. Because of the short tenure of most editors, knowledge about the place was passed on in almost another language, a jargon made up of shorthand references to predecessors and the manner of their going. Mercer found it hard to catch on, having no one to fill her in on the history of the cautionary tales they referred to.

She did catch on, quickly, to the omnipresence of the old man. The phones were bugged, she was told, the washrooms were bugged. Don't get caught speeding in this town, don't even risk a parking ticket. The locals report it to the old man right away. Don't drop your personal mail in with the office mail; his people in the mail room examine the mail, open private letters. Be careful of what you dispose of in the wastebasket. The cleanup crew go through the trash at night. Use the shredder—it's safer. The rules were numerous. "The work itself is only half of it," Mercer confided to her neighbor Susan. "It's the hassle of dealing with the other people in the office that gets me down."

Faster than she could have believed, the weekday routine became set. The clock radio gave a little click before it turned itself on. Mercer was generally half-awake before the click, an aura of apprehension toward the day ahead already gathering, like an invisible early morning mist blanketing her bed. She rose into anxiety through layers of sleep. "Here comes the sun," sang the Beatles as the radio warmed up, and Mercer opened her eyes to blazing dawns and dreary memos and deadline pressures.

Her hand would reach out and still the radio for another five minutes. She would turn her back to the sun and burrow in. But she had to get up and go to work. "We have to eat," she said, although she could not truly admit that she was afraid of going hungry. Such a fear had never touched her. She certainly did not feel hungry in the cool pink mornings, enjoying the comfort of her bed, the crisp sheets, lying in a doze, half-listening for the mullet to jump in the canal and the raucous voice of the great blue heron. Yes, life was okay, basically okay. She was ready to kick off the sheet; it lay too heavy when the sun began to warm the air. She was ready to yell for Benjamin to wake up. "Hit the deck! Breakfast! What do you want in your lunchbox?"

The job was a necessity. She had to work. More than food and shelter, it proved competency. Seriousness. When she received her paycheck, when she cashed it at the bank, when she exchanged the money for groceries or rent or paid the utility bills or bought a wire basket for Benjamin's second-hand bicycle, she knew that even so simple a life as the one she had would not be possible without a job. Still, she regretted that the work itself meant so little to her.

She had friends with jobs, but most of her friends seemed to take jobs simply to fill in time between other things. They weren't real jobs, because they weren't demanding. When Sarah had been divorced from her first husband, before she married again, she had had a job. Something at Lincoln Center. Coordinating a project, the Artists in Residence Program, something like that. And Ina, during her year of celibacy, had been into some very interesting things, like scouting films for Paramount . . . or was it Universal? Anyway, Mercer couldn't remember ever hearing Sarah or Ina talk about their work as if it were real labor. No. It was only an interesting activity that gave them something to talk about at parties.

Generally, her friends had husbands, the way some people might have careers. Harriet, for example, on marrying her third husband, a prominent writer and editor, after having been married to a Hungarian patriot and an animal psychologist, said, "I've never really had a husband before." And her friends, watching Harriet take her husband's journalistic career in hand, running his Manhattan home and his home in Ireland and his many children who became her stepchildren, and correcting his galleys, and entertaining the people who published or read him, understood exactly what she meant.

Mercer wondered if she should look for a different job, do something else, something she could learn from. If she had a true profession—if she were a teacher, a doctor, a lawyer—if she had a real job, would she feel differently about work? She did not think she could find another job in the area that would pay her as well. The newspaper was notorious for capturing its staff with high salaries. And then, perhaps every job was just a job on some level.

And was Cormack just a businessman? she asked herself. Just an ordinary, ambitious, self-absorbed businessman, running the family estate, watching the family's investments? Intent on having what he wanted, and able to afford it?

She used to think that businessmen spoke about their work with some irony that escaped her because she was an outsider, not a member of the club. Then at a dinner party she had heard a group of wealthy oil men discussing the chances of a cold winter. She could not detect a single trace of irony.

Would Charles Bronson take a businessman seriously? Wouldn't he, as Mercer now did, just take the paycheck?

She used to be apologetic in New York about not having worked. She had a set speech, in which she mentioned her lack of training, her early marriage, the baby that came so soon; then a little list of things she had done, showing how unimportant her efforts had been. "I never did anything but sell socialist newspapers in college, and work two weeks in a factory on a dare."

"You left out something," Cormack had said once, though he did not care if she ever did anything.

"What?"

"You've forgotten the time we were dining at Lutece and someone told you you couldn't make a living if you had to. You picked up the fruit from the centerpiece on the table and went around to the other tables selling it to the customers until you were able to pay your own portion of the bill with the profits."

He was right. She had stared at him, astounded, silenced for a moment. Of course, he was right, it fit right in, she would add it to her list and use it the next time she explained her lack of a résumé. "And," she had added, thinking of one more accomplishment, "I learned to type all by myself," but Cor had stopped listening. It was after that she had volunteered to work for the congressman and had finally felt useful and competent.

What if she did have some expertise to offer the world? Her formal education, now years behind her, had dropped away from her, as easily forgotten as the instructions for parsing a sentence or the ability to decide the properties of points, lines, angles, and figures in space. Now she sat at a desk and answered trivial questions. Judging by the success of the weekly tabloid she worked for, the public's appetite for trivia was insatiable. *I am drowning in trivia*, she thought. She picked up a blank query slip. "What would I like to know?" she asked. She took a pencil and began to fill it out.

What happened to Shelley's heart after Trelawny picked it out of the flames?

She filled in another.

If nitrogen is lighter than oxygen, why isn't all the nitrogen in the air floating on top of the oxygen?

They're not so different, she thought. My questions are not so different from any of the others. For the first time she understood the unslaked thirst of the paper's readers—the wish to know. Who is in love this week, who is getting a million dollars for a movie, who made a scene at a Beverly Hills restaurant? She had her own nosy set of inquiries. *I would read, avidly*, she admitted, *the most conjectural details about . . . oh, Edvard Munch, for example. I would read the dirty words that Virginia Woolf shouted into the bushes at the side of the road when she was mad. I would read the novel that Emily Bronte threw on the fire.*

All recorded facts, she decided, are somebody's trivia.

CHAPTER ELEVEN

Mercer worked steadily through the afternoon, trying to reduce the size of the stack of queries on her desk.

Who is the new man in Cher's life?

How many states have legalized Bingo?

Is Smokey the Bear still alive?

Is it ketchup or catsup?

Who decides whether a movie is X-rated?

How old is Soupy Sales?

What was Pavlov's dog's name?

Who cares? thought Mercer. Her desk was a clearinghouse for trivia. Yet the editors and reporters demanded the answers as if they were matters of life and death. She implored them to tell her the answer they were searching for, not just the question. "It makes it easier for me to know when I've found it," she explained—reasonably, she thought. But they were secretive. They hoped she could find the information they needed without having to tip their hands. Mercer was learning to cover herself by citing unimpeachable sources for every piece of information she gave. But if she had not divined their objective, she delivered an answer but implied that her search for further answers was continuing. "Cover yourself" was the name of the game throughout the company.

Halfway through the afternoon the inside telephone on Mercer's desk rang. It was squat and black and made a different sound from the outside phone, and, unlike the outside phone, it rang only once. She picked up the receiver and put it to her ear. There was no need for her to speak. "Come down," a sepulchral voice said. Henry David Finkelstein was wielding his new authority as managing editor with a vengeance. Everyone in the editorial office dreaded the sound of the inside telephone, everybody dreaded the voice, full of menace, and the simple command. There was never any explanation. The subject of the summons was never announced, so that she might come to the meeting supplied with documentation, or use the few seconds' walk down the corridor to the editorial department to collect her thoughts, muster her defenses.

Walking down the hall that led from the reference library to the newsroom, Mercer passed the publisher's private office just as the closed door opened and the owner of the newspaper came out. There was an awkward moment as she tried to change course and go around him and he tried the same maneuver.

She had seen him before, of course. One of the reporters had pointed him out to her. She was surprised at how ordinary he looked, like any middle-class businessman, in spite of the fact that his employees spoke of him as if he were a Borgia, full of threat and intrigue and malice. True, he had a habit of wearing dark, almost black sunglasses, even indoors, glasses that were more like the shield of a blind man than tinted glasses to hide eyes from the light. He was a tall man, with iron-gray hair that looked as if it were a week or two overdue for a cut, not as if it were deliberately styled long. His upper torso was heavy and barrel-shaped, and the aggressive thrust of his body as he maneuvered to avoid bumping into her confirmed her suspicion that he deliberately distanced himself from the people who worked for him. She sensed that if he had bumped into her, she would have been in jeopardy. Once she had inadvertently given his secretary a piece of erroneous information. She had corrected it five minutes later, but the next time she went out onto the editorial floor everybody there knew that she had given the boss the wrong answer. Still, until he made an overt gesture of power toward her, she intended to make no judgment. Cor had called her paranoid, but she intended to be the last holdout in the paranoid atmosphere of this office.

"Excuse me—good afternoon," she murmured, not loud enough for him to actually hear her words and possibly think that she expected a response. She did not. But she wanted to initiate some sort of exchange so that he would not think she was dumb. Or intimidated.

In the few weeks she had been there, she had not spoken directly to him. Any queries from his office were passed to her and back through one, or sometimes two, intermediaries. Still, she felt—as she knew by now that most people employed by the paper felt—that the old man knew, or could know if he wished to, everything about her. He could get hold of financial information, medical records. Her bank and her local doctor would no doubt be forthcoming. Members of the local police department worked for the old man in their spare time, as security guards and personal bodyguards. He would know if she got a ticket for a traffic offense. He probably knew that she was a registered Democrat, that she had a library card, that she rented rather than owned the house where she lived. In this small town, the man's power was ubiquitous. Just passing him in the hall was an event.

Mercer stopped on her way to Finkelstein's office to look at herself in the mirror in the ladies' room. If she set her jaw and frowned, she could almost capture Charles Bronson's glower. True, she didn't have the wrinkles to make it work, but the foreshadowings of deep lines were there. What she needed was a mask of defensiveness so cool that nobody would misread it. "Mercer," she said firmly to the face in the mirror. "The silence under the fist." She walked down the hall with a swagger.

The managing editor sat hunched over his desk, his bulky body leaning on his thin arms. He did not bother to look at her as he spoke.

"What?" she asked when he had finished his speech, realizing too late that she would now have to listen to a repetition of the charge.

"You have been accused of being too fond of ambiguity. It has been reported more than once.

Editors are complaining. They don't want an answer that can be understood in two different ways. It makes their work harder. They have to make decisions all the time. They need hard-edge answers. I think you've worked here long enough now to know what the score is. Never give an editor a reply that conveys subjectivity; never interpret his question; keep asking the question until you get the answer the editor wants."

He paused. "The next ambiguous answer you give to a query may well be your last."

She stood silent in the face of his threat. All she could think was, *yes, it's true. I am fond of ambiguity, I really am.*

"In addition, you've been demoted."

"Demoted!" She was startled. "To what? From what?"

"You have been demoted in title and responsibility. This will be posted on the bulletin board. You were Chief Researcher. You are now Assistant Researcher."

"But there's only one person in my department. How could I be either chief or assistant?"

Finkelstein dismissed her abruptly as his secretary delivered a pizza box to his desk. Mercer realized that she had ceased to exist for him, even as she stood there.

Back at her desk, she looked first for a message from Benjamin. He should have checked in with her by now. It was Monday, the only day he did not have an after-school activity that kept him occupied until the time she got home from the office. Tuesdays and Thursdays, he had ball practice on the school grounds; Wednesdays, he went to an art class at the civic center, next door to the school; and on Fridays, he went to story hour at the public library.

Her anxiety increased as the afternoon waned. Both telephones on her desk rang constantly, but there was no call from Benjamin to say he was home from school.

He walked home from school every day now that she was working, accompanied most of the way by other children. He let himself in with his key on a shoelace around his neck like any latch-key kid. Mercer had painted her office telephone number above the kitchen phone and had showed him how to dial. The routine was for him to call to say that he was home. She would ask about his day at school while it was still fresh in his mind. She would tell him to have a glass of milk or eat an apple and remind him to put his books away. Then he would go next door and say hello to Susan and play in the Peale's fenced-in yard with the new litter of puppies. Twice there had been a hitch in their routine. Once Benjamin had played in the school yard until the fading light reminded him to go home. Once he had lost his key and had to sit on the front step until Mercer came home from work.

She dialed her home number, wondering if Benjamin had tried to call when her telephone was tied up and had become discouraged by the busy signals. As she listened to the steady rings, a reporter walked in and made out a query slip.

"I'm in a hurry for this," he said. "Very rush."

She sighed and hung up and read the two questions on the query slip.

Do you have to be dead to be a saint?

What is the clinical definition of death?

She looked at the reporter. She debated asking him what the thrust of his story was to be.

She called the Apostolic See in Washington and took down a simple definition of sainthood that the reporter, reading over her shoulder and nodding, could evidently use. Next she pulled the medical dictionaries down from the shelves and opened them to the word "death."

"There are a lot of definitions," she said to him, pointing to the page. "Apparent death, black death, brain death, cell death, crib death, liver death, local death, molecular death, somatic death. I don't see 'clinical death,' but here's a general definition that should cover it—'legal death: The irreversible cessation of all the following: One, total cerebral function; two, spontaneous function of the respiratory system; and three, spontaneous function of the circulatory system.' " She knew as she spoke that she was breaking another of Finkelstein's rules—giving more information than had been requested. "Won't that suit your purposes? I think the legal definition must be pretty close to the clinical definition."

The reporter looked at her suspiciously. "How so?" he asked.

"How not?" she responded.

She knew she was in for it before the reporter stamped out of the room. He was going to complain about her lack of cooperation to Finkelstein.

She hoped that Henry David was still occupied with his pizza and would not have time to listen. She quickly dialed her home telephone number once more. Poor Benjamin, was he locked out again?

Suppose Cormack has found us again? Mercer asked herself. Driving home as fast as she dared in the rush hour traffic on Interstate 95, she remembered what Quinn had said to her: "Contact no one, no one. Not your best friend, not your old nurse, no relatives. Cut all ties. It will be someone close to you who gives you away. Not even meaning to. Someone who is careless, or forgetful. Or just mentions you to a friend who later mentions you to a third party, who happens to tell your husband. If you are going to do it, do it right."

Why had she called Sarah, why hadn't she ripped the telephone from the wall before she did such a thing? Cormack might have heard already, he might even be here. Oh, don't let it be so, she begged, driving as fast as she could. And don't let it be me who led Cormack here.

Quinn had searched old newspapers and microfiche until he found the name of someone who had died as a child at about the time Mercer was born. Even the name was not so different from her maiden name. With the name and the parents' names Quinn had found, Mercer had gone to the bureau of vital statistics to order a copy of the child's birth certificate. Then she had taken the birth certificate to the Post Office and applied for a Social Security number. "No," she had said, "I never had

one before. I have never worked. The only thing
I ever did was to sell socialist newspapers in college
and . . ."

She took the birth certificate and the Social Security card to the voters' registration office and
applied for a voter's card in the new name. With
these three pieces of identification, she took her
driver's test over again and got a new driver's license. Each time she obtained new documents, she
had them mailed to Quinn's office, not to herself.

"Move to another state," Quinn had instructed
her. That did not mean, he amended, moving to
Cape Cod or Georgetown or Westport. "To reduce
the possibility of accidentally running into someone you know, move to an area that people you
know don't visit."

He continued. "Don't put your son in a private
school. Unless you strongly feel that he should
receive an elitist education, go ahead and send him
to public school. There's also something to be
gained from the experience of sharing the common
condition.

"Break off all contact with relatives, family doctors and lawyers, and friends. A skilled investigator
can use sophisticated pretexts that will deceive
even the most alert friends. Those closest to you
could inadvertently betray you."

"Can I call you? Sometime?"

He looked at her. "No."

He was silent for a while. "Okay, what else do
we have? I'd advise you to change your vocation,
but you don't have one. You are not likely to get
tripped up that way.

"Do you have any hobbies? Do you collect anything, subscribe to anything, contribute to anything? Leave it all behind. Do you excel at anything? Golf, tennis? Drop it.

"Have you ever had your fingerprints taken? If your fingerprints are on file anywhere, don't get a job that requires giving them again."

Mercer shook her head. She hated having her picture taken. She hated being ID'd, being labeled. It had always seemed an invasion of privacy to be forced to give up one's fingerprints. Like having your secrets known. She had done a tour of Washington, D.C., as a high school student, but when the class was ushered through the FBI building she had not let them take her fingerprints. "No, thank you," she had said politely.

"Don't do anything that draws attention to yourself. Don't sue anybody. Don't get sued. Don't run for office. Don't become important."

He was still looking at her. "Your appearance."

"What?"

"The way you look. Can you change . . . a little?"

"How?"

"Cut your hair. Wear glasses. You have such a special . . . such a definite look. Can't you change it a little?"

She could see that he did not really want her to change. "Don't worry," she said. "I'll blend in with the scenery, wherever I am." She told him that she did not believe she was distinctive looking.

She did not tell him that until she was nearly grown she had no clear idea of what she looked like. It was not looking in mirrors that left me not knowing, she thought. In my family, vanity was forbidden.

She had thought that she had a face like a sun bear's, with all the features in the front. In high school biology class she learned that such a characteristic among mammals has a name; it is called "dish-faced." The expression struck her with anguish and spoiled her self-image that difficult year. It was not until she was seventeen, trying on a dress in a department store in a spacious dressing room with multiple mirrors that she saw her own profile for the first time.

She told Quinn about it. "I had a nose! A real nose—a beak!—not at all what I supposed my nose looked like. I had a profile. What a surprise! Not bad!" She laughed. Not bad, as she got older and the bones refined down; not bad in the summer when the sun streaked her hair and burnished the smooth skin across her high cheekbones.

She was so late coming into these looks, however, that it was actually Sarah and Grace, after Benjamin was born, who told her she was beautiful. "True," Ina agreed, "in spite of the fact that Mercer sometimes looks as if she is dragging her life along behind her like a deadweight."

She could see that Quinn could only think of her looking the way she looked now, the way she was. "I can wear my hair pulled back," she told him. "And go back to wearing my glasses. I don't like contacts, anyway. I will dress differently. I am taking none of my things with me. I'll change in lots of ways, I'll be somebody different. Truly, Quinn, I'll be so careful. . . ."

But she had not been careful enough. She had called Sarah. Homesick, mellow with the smoke and the wine, she had called Sarah for a gossip. For the familiar spin of talk. Had Sarah told Grace, had Grace mentioned it to her husband, had Charles dropped a word at his club, had Cor finally picked up the news that she had called? But she hadn't said anything, not anything, had she, to give away where she was?

"Don't let it be so," she said again as she pulled into her driveway. But there was no small boy sitting on the doorstep. There was nobody there at all.

CHAPTER TWELVE

Sarah launched into a nonstop monologue the moment she heard Mercer's voice on the line. Mercer let her ramble on, using the time to collect her thoughts.

"Let me see," Sarah was saying. "I suppose that the most exciting thing that's happened since I spoke to you last is that Grace saved that monster Charles from choking to death. She employed the Heimlich maneuver. We were all at a dinner party at Charles's mother's—you know her, Ondine, the dress designer. It was a very elegant party. Ondine asked Charles to fetch something from the desk in the hall—something she wanted to show to one of the guests. Now, Mercy, picture this: Ondine asks Charles to go and get whatever it is. He tucks a bit of tournedos into his cheek to sustain him on the trip. Then, in the foyer, he begins to choke on it. At first he coughs discreetly. Then he realizes that it isn't working. He needs to get a breath to cough harder, but he can't because he has used up all his breath being discreet. He starts back toward the dining room. He falls to his knees. Grace looks up from her asparagus and notices her husband crawling in from the butler's pantry. She sits still for a second. Then she murmurs, 'Excuse me,' puts her napkin beside her plate, and rises from the table. She walks over to Charles, places herself on her knees over his back, and grasps him around the diaphragm. Then she quickly and efficiently expels the piece of meat. A heroine!

"I said to her later, after we had left the table, 'Why didn't you let him die?'

" 'As soon as I saw he was all right,' Grace said, 'that's exactly what I asked myself: Now, why didn't I just let nature take its course? But it was something I wanted to do,' Grace said. She said it vindicated her sense of eternal readiness. It was sort of like acting out that dream of being called upon to save someone—that dream of plucking your child from the sea, or jumping in front of the speeding car. You know that dream, Mercer, we've all had that dream.''

"And Cor was there?" Mercer finally interrupted. She had to track Cor's movements.

"Yes, yes, all the old crowd. Oh, and guess who—"

"And this was yesterday? Yesterday? Or the day before?"

"Last night, darling. That's why I'm still so full of it."

If Cor had been at a dinner party last night, did it mean that Benjamin might be lost, really lost? Taken into some stranger's house where a little boy had been wanted for a long time? Fallen into a canal? "Sarah, you haven't mentioned to Cor that I called you that time?"

"Not a word."

"Did you tell anyone? Anyone?"

"No, Mercy, truly. Are you all right? Is there anything I can do?"

"No. I've got a bit of an emergency here. I have to hang up in a minute. I just wanted to find out if Cor is in the city and ask you if you had told anybody about my call. And I wanted to ask about Ina. How is she?"

"They say that she's in remission. They say that it is not life-threatening, that it is in her bones, that she will live for quite a while. I know that I will see you again, Mercer, wherever you are, but when I haven't seen Ina for a few days, I panic."

"I know. Give her my love. But don't mention this call to anyone else. I have to hang up, Sarah."

"Take care."

The call confirmed Mercer's guess that it was not Cormack this time. It hadn't felt like it; she had had no sense of his approach, of his being anywhere near. But if it wasn't Cormack, where was Benjamin?

She would try one more thing before she called the police. She would go up and down the lane, asking those neighbors who were at home if they had seen Benjamin during the afternoon.

Susan Peale seemed not quite able to take in the situation. "I wasn't around all day. I had somewhere I had to be—an appointment I had to keep. I mean, I didn't have to keep it, but I decided to. So I didn't get back until about three-thirty, but Ben didn't come by anyway. I missed him, because I usually let him feed the puppies and take Maggie on the leash up and down the lane for a little walk.

But I didn't really worry about it when he didn't show up, because sometimes he'd rather play or have a snack. Is there anything I can do?"

"Listen for my telephone while I walk over to Johntie's and through to the next street. I just want to ask whether anybody saw him on the way home. Please, Susan—thanks. The phone's on the wall in the kitchen."

Johntie was sitting on the steps of his small efficiency, dangling colored threads from his fingers as he wrapped the handle of a fishing pole in a complex geometric pattern. She explained to him that Benjamin was lost and that she was searching for him. The alarm in his eyes showed her that he understood even though he couldn't hear the way her voice was trembling.

"I will come with you," he said in his low, husky voice that was so even in tone, it was almost totally lacking in inflection.

"No," she said. "Not now. I will ask you later if I need you."

Mercer looked down the empty lane. She had to call the police. Briney Breezes was such a small town; if Benjamin was lost, he would be quickly found. She would not raise the possibility of kidnapping with the police—not yet. It could not jeopardize Ben's safety to keep quiet about the past for a little longer. And she had a strong feeling that it was not Cormack this time. The day had been oppressively full of anxiety, but she had not once felt that Cor was catching up with them again. She had been so careful. It was hard to believe that another round of warfare between

herself and Cormack could begin, after all the pre-
cautions she had taken, the good start she had
made.

She hurried back down the lane. Now that it
was threatened, she loved life in the small town
house that sat like a new box on the bank of the
canal. She loved the routine her life had fallen into,
the leggy heron that woke her in the morning, the
sense of purpose in going to work every day, the
earned freedom of the weekends. She and Ben had
a life here. *Please don't make us start all over again*,
she prayed. *Please let me have Benjamin while he's
a child—Cormack can have him when he's thirty*. The
idea of Benjamin, with his skinny nape and baby
fingers, being thirty, almost made her smile.

She sent Susan home before she made the telephone call to the police. She would not mention
the question of kidnapping at all. What could the
local police do? A small-town law enforcement
squadron with their limited resources. It would be
just as Quinn had described it—the police would
not go beyond their own jurisdiction.

But what could be done here and now would
be done. She had to ask them for help. They would
do the things they did best. If Benjamin was somewhere in this small town, they would find him. If
all her instincts were wrong and Cor had taken
him again, she would deal with that later. For the
moment, she must take things one at a time and
try to think as clearly as she could.

She dialed the Briney Breezes Police Department. In a calm and organized way she explained
to the sergeant at the desk that her little boy had

not come home from school. The man took her name, address, and telephone number and told her that he was dispatching a squad car to her home; the car was out on patrol not far from her neighborhood, he said. It would be there almost immediately.

Waiting was impossible. She looked over into Susan's yard, but it was dark and there seemed to be no one at home, unless Susan was sitting there with all the lights off. She went back into her own kitchen and called the school, wondering if there had been some accident that she had not been informed of. But the school had her home and office telephone numbers; surely she would have been notified earlier.

There was no reply. The school was closed.

She heard the police car brake and turn into the gravel drive. Two men came to the door. They were not in uniform, yet gave the impression of being in uniform anyway. They had a formal air that made them seem discomfited, almost abashed. Why not, she thought, we are strangers after all. They introduced themselves. She began, hoping to put them at ease.

"I am Mercer Ramsey. I called you. My little boy didn't come home after school today. He goes to Briney Breezes Elementary School. He was supposed to walk home by himself today. I called from the office where I work, several times, but there was never an answer. There's no sign that he came home and then went out to play. And I know that he had his key today, I remember checking with him this morning."

"Who lives here, besides yourself and your son?"

"Just the two of us."

"What is his usual routine? Does he ever go home with a friend to play?"

"No. We are rather new—he doesn't know any children well enough to go home with them. Although there's always a first time. . . ." Her voice rose hopefully. Could Benjamin have gone home with some other child?

"Does he know how to dial your number, Mrs. Ramsey?"

"My number?"

"Your home number, here. Does he know how to dial it? Has he ever dialed it himself?"

"Actually, no. He calls me at the office, we practiced that and he checks in with me every day. But he has never called here." She looked at the telephone as if it might ring at any minute. "He has just learned to dial."

"What about Mr. Ramsey?"

"Who?" she asked stupidly, caught off guard.

"What about your husband? Does he live in the area? Should he be notified?"

Mercer tried to think fast. Why hadn't she thought of an answer beforehand?

"He's dead."

The two policemen were silent.

"Do you think," she suggested, "if I went with you over the route from school . . . we might see something that attracted his attention, or some—some hazard, something."

"Later," the man said. "Do you have a picture of . . . what did you call the boy?"

"Benjamin, Ben." She gestured toward the photograph on the shelf, the one of Benjamin in the big blue velvet chair, holding up his ball of bubble gum.

"Another one? A school picture?"

"Oh, yes." She fumbled in her bag. "Here's one, a school picture. You can see . . . brown eyes, brown hair."

"How old is the boy, Mrs. Ramsey?"

"Six."

"How tall?"

She put her hand out from her waist, palm down as if touching Ben's hair. "About . . . this high." She jerked her hand away and began to stalk nervously around the room. "Shouldn't we be . . . I don't know, going through the streets, asking people questions?"

"Things are being done, Mrs. Ramsey."

"What things?"

"All the routine things. We are checking all the playgrounds in the area, all the empty lots, the canals, the swimming pools."

"The swimming pools," she echoed faintly. "He can swim . . . pretty well for his age."

"In an area like this, we always check them first. We've contacted Mr. Goode, the principal of the school. He is going around with the custodian. He told us that the boy was in school today—"

"Of course he was in school! I took him there myself!" Mercer heard her voice going up. Remember your speech lessons. If you let your voice get higher and higher it will turn into a scream and then it will just disappear.

The policeman went on calmly. "Mr. Goode will provide us with telephone numbers. Who are some of your son's classmates?"

Mercer drew a blank. "He talks about a boy named Andy. And someone he sits next to—Billy, I think. May I go with you?"

Mr. Goode was concerned. Worried. He had a street map spread across his desk. The air-conditioning had been turned off. In his suit and tie, he was melting in the warm evening air. "Through that way?" he was saying. "No, no. None of the children go home that way. That route would take them right through Century Acres. You know, none of the children go that way. You know, Gleason." He turned to one of the detectives. "They cross at Main Street, the school crossing guard crosses them there. And then the children who live in the northeast section of town—I think you'll find this is true, Mrs. Ramsey—these children walk down Miner Road, through the Greenacres development—five or six of them live there—and then onto Northeast Tenth. None of them live in Century Acres, of course, so none of them walk through there. They cut east, and then north again, and pretty soon all the children who are within walking distance are at home. The bus route picks up after that." He came to the end of the geography lesson and looked up at her.

"But Benjamin and I worked out the route together," she said. "The way we walked seemed the shortest way."

Mr. Goode shook his head. His finger started again at the beginning, tracing the way from school, across Main Street, down Miner Road, across the oak surface of his desk. Sergeant Gleason agreed. "I've been here ten years, and I never see the kids from school going through that section."

In the last light of dusk, Mercer rode in the squad car with the two men who seemed already to have become her companions. They drove slowly through the dusty lanes of the town.

"Why?" she asked. "Why do the children go this way around? It's much farther and much less direct."

"The people in these retirement communities —and Century Acres is not the only one—are very hostile toward young people and children. They don't like to pay school taxes, and they refuse to be taxed for civic improvements such as parks and playgrounds. Sometimes a kid will try to speed through the area on a bicycle, just raising hell. He'll usually get chased out by a cane-waving senior citizen. And kids avoid the area on Halloween. But there have been more serious incidents too."

"What do you mean by serious?"

"A year or so ago a family with two young children moved in there. It is a retirement community, and has exclusionary renting laws, but this couple had inherited the house from the woman's elderly parents, and instead of selling it back to the corporation, they moved in themselves.

"In December, their home was broken into and vandalized. Their Christmas tree was knocked over, and I believe some of the presents under the tree were stolen. The family was on the receiving end of a lot of threats and telephone calls too. They finally moved away—left the state, I believe."

"Are the elderly really that militant?"

"Well, they have a defense. They say that they settled here for peace and quiet in their old age, and that they should be entitled to create the kind of community they choose. They say that ethnic and religious groups and the rich and the poor have their enclaves, why can't they have theirs? They don't want to pay high property taxes on their retirement incomes. Last year, senior citizens got an ordinance passed that gives communities the right to include restrictive covenants in property deeds barring children. That's how Century Acres can make it illegal for persons under eighteen to live there except during brief visits or under special circumstances."

"But how sad never to see children!" Mercer said.

The detective shrugged. "They don't figure it that way."

The squad car came to the end of Northeast Tenth Street, where Century Acres began, behind its gate and with its twin black cannons aimed at the outside world. The car turned onto U.S. 1. They had seen nothing more than a small town closing down for the night. Mercer wondered if they had driven her around just to satisfy her need to do something.

"What now?" she asked.

"There's nothing more you can do on this end tonight. Go home and stay by the telephone. Look around the house and see if there is any indication that the boy came home and left again. Is there anybody who can stay with you? We can send a female officer over. Or maybe you'd like to ask a neighbor in."

Mercer realized that whatever the forces of justice would be doing through the long night ahead, she was about to be abandoned to get through it the best way she could.

"What are you going to be doing?" she asked bluntly.

"We will be working on this through the night. We'll be cooperating with the local newspaper and radio. We have the routine things we do, and then we'll be at the school when it opens."

"You'll call me no matter what time if—"

"We will send someone over to your house if there is any news. But don't expect too much tonight. We need the daytime to do most of the things we do—house to house inquiries, checking the shops along Main Street, and so forth."

"What time—how early can I call you tomorrow?"

"Well, I myself won't be on duty. I will have handed the case over to the next shift. But the work will go on, of course. Call as early as you want. Give your name to the man on dispatch. You'll reach someone on the case."

The case, she thought.

She suddenly felt as if she were only half-conscious of what she was doing or saying, as if she had been in a half-faint since she had discovered that Benjamin was missing. She was afraid she had been only half as quick and decisive as she needed to be, and that she was nowhere near strong enough to get through the next few hours.

CHAPTER THIRTEEN

She was with the police for an hour, for two hours. They accompanied her home and searched again all the places she had already looked. Finally they left her. Do you want a policewoman to stay? they asked again. No, I have neighbors, she replied. But for the moment she was alone with her thoughts.

The house seemed just the way she and Benjamin had left it that morning. She stood at the bottom of the stairs, looking at the jumbled piles of things in the corner of each step. Most of the objects had been there all week, she thought. There was a skateboard. Crayons. An inflated ball from the last trip to the beach. A stack of clean towels waiting to be taken upstairs and stored in the linen closet. Nothing missing here—the piles simply grew from day to day. She picked up a handful of things to carry up.

In the upstairs hall she found more scattered objects, but she decided they had all been there for several days.

I think I'd know if a toy were missing, she thought. *I'd certainly know if T-shirts and socks and shorts were gone*. She bent and picked up a handful of small boy's clothing, and remembered a time when she was doing the same thing in the New York apartment, picking up a long trail of blocks and soldiers, toys that marked a path to the door of Benjamin's room like Hansel and Gretel's crumbs. Bending and picking up and putting away, she had half-listened to Cor's voice within as he told Benjamin—had he been just four then?—a bedtime story.

"What's it going to be tonight, Daddy?"

"One of Aesop's fables," Cor decided. "Come on, tuck your feet in. Now. Once upon a time there was a little boy who was sent out to watch over the sheep at night."

"Didn't he have to go to bed?"

"He was old enough to stay up late. Anyway, the boy became lonely all by himself on the hillside, and—"

"Daddy, why couldn't two boys watch the sheep?"

"How should I know? Perhaps there weren't enough boys in the village, and they had to take turns."

"Were there any girls?"

"This boy that I am telling the story about was alone, and he thought of a wicked plan to get company. He called out, 'Wolf! Wolf!' and all the people of the village came running."

"That's not a wicked plan. That's a very good plan," came Ben's wide-awake but puzzled voice.

"Well, the people were very angry at being disturbed for nothing, and they went back to their homes. But within half an hour, the boy called out again, 'Wolf! Wolf!' "

"Why didn't they—" Ben began.

"You aren't listening for the main point of the story," Cor said disapprovingly. "The people were very angry and told the boy not to dare call out again. So the boy sat on the hillside with the sheep. But soon a wolf really did come. And the boy called out, 'Wolf! Wolf! Help! Help!' But no one believed him this time. And no one came to help him. And the wolf ate up all the sheep."

"He wouldn't do that," Benjamin assured his father. "One wolf wouldn't eat up all the sheep. He would kill one sheep and fill his belly and carry the rest back to his babies. I saw it on television."

There was a long silence in the room. Mercer was all ears. So far she preferred Benjamin's version.

"I'll tell you another story," said Cormack.

"Oh, goody. What's it about?"

"It's one I learned at Harvard Business School. But like all good stories, it applies to real life too. Every business executive knows this story. Here goes. It's called The Hawthorne Experiment.

"Once upon a time, there were six ladies who worked in a factory. Every day they went to the factory and worked, and every day was just the same as the day before. That was called phase one.

"Then the managers began an experiment. They put the women in a special room all by themselves. Output increased a little."

"What does that mean, Daddy?"

"It means they worked a little harder. They made more things. That was phase two.

"In phase three, their pay rate was changed, so it was based on the average of just their little group, not the average of the whole plant. Production went up.

"In phase four, they invented the coffee break. History in the making. They gave the ladies two rest breaks of five minutes each, one in the morning and one in the afternoon. Production went up.

"In phase five, the ladies were given six rest breaks of five minutes each. They complained that it was distracting. Production remained the same."

Benjamin interrupted, bored. "What's going to happen, Daddy?" Mercer was wondering too.

"It goes on like this for a bit," Cor replied. "In phase six, the rest breaks were changed again. A fifteen minute break in the morning and ten minutes in the afternoon, with the company providing refreshments. Doughnuts," he defined for Benjamin. This time Ben joined him and they chanted together: "Production went up!"

"In phase seven, the workday was stopped at 4:30 P.M. Production went up!

"In phase eight, work stopped at four P.M. Production went up!"

"The experts were amazed by now. They went back to phase four and repeated it. Did production drop back to phase-four level?" Cor paused, but his audience was silent. "No, production again went up," he announced.

"In phase ten, the work week was reduced from five and a half days to five. Production went up.

"Phase eleven was a return to phase three: No

rest breaks, no refreshments, old working hours. Production fell off slightly, then started to increase again.

"Phase twelve was a repeat of phase six. Two coffee breaks. Production rose dramatically. By now output had increased by more than twenty-five percent! What did it all mean? What is the main point of this story?"

Mercer could hear Benjamin wiggling and sitting up in bed, stuttering. He always tried, with Cor, to get the main point.

Cor cut him off short. "It means that if you give everybody just a little attention, they'll all feel important, and they'll all do what you want them to do."

Oh, no, Cor, she thought. *That's not a story you tell a child.*

There was silence from his audience. Mercer figured that Benjamin, who by now knew what form a story took, was probably trying to figure out whether his father's narrative was really a story after all. She remembered a man, a physicist, she had met the week before at an opera benefit. He had told her that he had learned everything he knew of the lives of men and women, everything he knew of emotions, from opera. Had Cor learned everything he knew of the human heart from Harvard Business School? Had he been programmed to think of people as productive or nonproductive units? Was it any worse—or any better—than learning about life from an efficiency expert? Her father had told her the same sort of cautionary tales about wasting time. God help students, she thought.

Mercer had walked into Benjamin's room then, her arms full of toys. "Are you trying to radicalize him or recruit him for Wall Street?"

"Neither one," Cor said. "It's my favorite story. Your father would like that story, bless his time-and-motion-study heart."

"I'm sure he would," she replied, thinking, *you both have always been interested only in the malleability of others. What I like is the capacity of personality to return to its original true form.*

Benjamin ran to the bathroom and back to show off his clean teeth, and Mercer lingered to talk and hum and tuck him in, hoping that he had been bored by the story, hoping he would forget it before he went to sleep. She wondered as she left Benjamin's bedroom and turned toward the wing where she and Cormack slept if her turn for a little attention was next on Cor's schedule.

In the house on the canal, Mercer counted Benjamin's stuffed toys and looked through the wooden chest where his clean clothes were kept. There was nothing missing, she was sure. If Cormack had taken Ben, would he leave her in suspense this long? What would be the point? She gazed blankly at a wall where Benjamin had painted a rainbow and labeled it "RAMBOW" in tall, shaky first-grade letters.

Downstairs, there was a noise.

Mercer hurried down the narrow stairs, facing

the dark rectangle of the wide glass doors at the back of the house. She turned toward the front door, but the sound repeated itself at the rear. Her first thought was of the bird at the window again, flying blindly in the dark. But a man stood there, his arms held so high that his jacket was strained wide as he leaned against the glass, one arm outspread against the window, the other crooked to make a shadowed hole so that he could peer into the dim interior. She could see him quite clearly. He was a large fair-haired man with wide hips and blank light eyes.

She flipped on the terrace lights and opened the door slightly, glaring in outrage. "Who are you? What do you want?"

"I tried the front door, but I couldn't get any response," he said apologetically. She frowned. It was possible that, upstairs, she had not heard. "So I came around to the back door to see if anybody was home. Back doors are friendlier, anyway, don't you think so, ma'am?"

She said nothing, waiting. He took a deep breath and began all over again.

"Good evening, Mrs . . . Ramsey." He hesitated expectantly, as if waiting for southern hospitality to lead to the next step.

"Yes, what is it?"

"Joe Dan Stephens," he declared. "Just stopped by on my way home. I work in the office of your automobile insurance company, Southern Federal. Something came up about your insurance, and I thought I'd try to clear it up. Knew you wouldn't want anything to go wrong on that, am I right? Won't take but a minute." He held out a business card.

"No, no—not now," she said, but he pushed past her on a tide of talk. He was a tall, middle-aged man with a heavy Swedish jaw. "Joe Dan Stephens," he introduced himself again. She did not invite him farther than the foyer and did not invite him to sit down. He seemed not to notice and stood near the table, absorbed in spreading some papers out on it.

"Now," he said, "there is some confusion in the records here. The question is, have you been insured before? Were you in 1972, 1974 maybe, driving a Porsche which was insured by Hartford Fidelity? Those darn computers, you know, they kick out these figures, and you can't argue back. Just have to take what the computer says and go check it out."

"That's impossible," Mercer said. "It must be someone else, there's no connection." She remembered Quinn's words: "No operator will find you now. Only bad luck or your own loneliness can catch you now." "No," she repeated, "you must be mistaken." She was rigid with tension but still hoped to dismiss the man casually. *Oh, God, if he would just go!*

There was a light, persistent tapping at the glass doors. "Excuse me," Mercer said.

She walked to the back door, thinking, *I know there is no connection, that stuff about the computer is nonsense. It's a pretext. But he doesn't look like the kind of private investigator that Cormack would hire.*

Cor always has anyone he deals with researched first, so that he'll know he's getting the best. Maybe this time the job has been farmed out, at least once, maybe twice. To the southern branch. The second-rate, third-rate southern operative.

Through the glass door she could see Johntie standing in the pale light that spilled out of the room onto the patio. She slid the door open. "Ben?" he asked, watching her face.

"No, not yet." She put her fingers against her lips and indicated the room behind her, so that he would realize there was someone there and keep his voice moderated.

"I came to find out if there is anything I can do," Johntie said in his rapid combination of sign language and speech. "Would you like me to sit with you? Make coffee?"

"Not now." She patted his shoulder gratefully. "But come in. Sit down. Wait." She pointed to a chair and returned to the man still standing beside the table. "He is a neighbor of mine," she explained. "He is deaf. He will wait until your business is finished."

"Well," the man said, trying to smile engagingly, "this won't take long." He shifted his heavy thighs, but Mercer resisted the hint that she might ask him to sit down. She had hated him at first sight. He had an irritating way of asking a question, then letting his face fall into an attitude of goofy attention, his head lolling back on his neck, his mouth falling open as if he used it for hearing.

She remembered an exercise a teacher had once

set for composition class, to teach the students to
develop a character who was unsympathetic. "In
the end, you must have sympathy for your villain
too," the professor had lectured. "Summon up the
worst person you can think of, and then think of
that person getting ready for bed. Mentally, step
by step . . . take his clothes off; find him a night-
shirt; pull up the blanket and tuck him in. Afterward, how can you feel so hateful about him,
ever?" She zipped through the exercise quickly.
But it did not change her attitude. She still disliked
Joe Dan Stephens. She particularly hated the
man's knowing and using her name.

"You've come at a very bad time, Mr. Stephens," she said. "I can't go into your problem
now, whatever it is." Still, she wondered why he
had really come and how long it would take to
find out.

"Just have a seat for a moment." The man
turned the tables on her by drawing up an arm-
chair for her, and Mercer suddenly, hardly meaning to, collapsed into it. This day, this dreadful day,
was taking its toll.

"Insurance rates," the man began, "are based
to some extent on the driver's record. Now, we
are insuring you as a new driver, but is that actually correct? Haven't you had a license before
. . . under another name, maybe?"

"No," she said flatly. And waited.

"Well, now, let me ask it this way." In spite of
his down-to-earth manner, the man had not the
slightest idea how to be affable. "Before you and

your little boy moved here, what kind of car were you driving?"

"My little boy?" She dropped her hand over the side of the chair and turned to see if Johntie was watching. He was looking at her, but she could tell he was making no attempt to follow the conversation by reading their lips. She could feel ice forming in her chest, and made an effort to keep her tone conversational. "What about my little boy? How did you know I have a little boy?" Over the side of the chair, concealed from the man, she spelled on her hand the word E-N-E-M-Y. Johntie went stock-still. She could tell he was alert, although he made no move. B-E C-A-R-E-F-U-L, she added.

"Why," said the man, "why, you remember we asked, for the forms, who else was in the family, who might be driving the car. I believe you mentioned then—"

"No, I don't believe I did." She watched him founder. If Cormack could see his local agent . . .

Johntie had drifted over to stand near a shelf, looking at a collection of shells. He moved toward the other corner of the table, but not out of sight of her busy hand.

H-E M-A-Y H-U-R-T B-E-N.

"Well, then, I guess I just knew, the way folks in a small town sort of know, or maybe I just guessed from the picture over there on the shelf."

She looked up, startled, at the photograph on the shelf. Benjamin was only four in that picture; the mysterious pinkish ball obscured part of his

face. "No," she said evenly. "It won't do. Where
is he?" Rage leaped into her voice. She gripped
the edge of the table. "Tell me where he is! I could
let the police make you tell. But I am in a hurry.
I want to know now. Where is he?"

The man was gaping at her, his eyes round. Her
voice rose, increased in volume, but it did not go
up and up and disappear. She said again, "Where
is he? Where have you got him? You'd better tell
me!" She pounded the table in front of him, her
jaws actually snapping with rage. Anger suffused
her chest like passion, and she felt it running in
her veins. She knew that nothing could stop her
from making this man tell her what she wanted
to know.

He rose clumsily from his chair, trying to shake
off her grip on his arm. "I don't know what you're
talking about, lady. I just came here to get some
forms straightened out, just doing my job." He
resorted to anger himself, in an attempt to quench
hers. "Look here, you must be some kind of crazy
lady. I don't know what's eating you. What are
you, some kind of nut? I didn't even know you
had a little boy."

"Then why did you ask me about him? How
did you recognize his picture?"

He began to stammer, looking apprehensively
into the impassive face of Johntie, who had moved
a step closer.

"What is this, anyhow?" he howled, jerking
away from the table and scattering the papers with
his heavy hand. He flopped in one direction and
then in another. He turned to look at the photo-

graph again, reaching for it. Just before his fingers closed around the frame, Mercer crashed the Queen Anne candlestick into one side of his skull, and Johntie clipped him on the other side with the flat blade of his fishing knife.

The man fell slowly, without a sound.

CHAPTER FOURTEEN

Mercer was still trying to think of some way to revive the man when the doorbell rang. The figure lying at her feet did not move. She certainly had not meant for this to happen. She had not been sure of herself when the moment came to act, not at all. She could actually have stood the man's company a while longer, now that she had a moment to think about it. Another five minutes, another ten minutes of questioning might have made everything different. Had Charles Bronson ever hit the wrong man? At the wrong time? This poor lump at her feet had been reaching for something on the shelf. The photograph of Benjamin. Maybe he'd only meant to straighten it, tidy it. Maybe something had offended his sense of alignment. If she had taken the time to think, would she ever actually have smashed someone who might be able to tell her where Benjamin was?

She bent and put her hand to his neck, but it felt like dry bread. Johntie lifted an eyelid, then jerked his hand back when the blank eye transfixed him, like the African pompano he had fought on the deck of the drift-fishing boat.

"What shall we do with him?" she asked Johntie, turning up her palms in a questioning gesture. She let herself believe the worst: The man was dead. This was where the events of the past year had been leading. This was what she had hardened herself to do. Yet it was impossible to accept that there was anything inevitable about the man lying at her feet.

The adrenaline rush of rage and fear faded, leaving her hollow and trembling. Nothing was changed, nothing solved. Violence had not enhanced the moment in any way; it had been as tedious and awkward as any act of living or dying. Was this the secret Charles Bronson hinted at on the screen? Did this explain his long reluctance to strike out, waiting until patience like a living membrane stretched as far as living tissue could allow? She looked down at Joe Dan Stephens, curled on his side, clad in a limp striped seersucker suit, indeed ready for bed, as she had, in her imagination, prepared him.

Johntie bent down and rearranged the slack body, making it somehow more compact, more of a bundle. He maneuvered the body toward the wicker couch, which was set across the center of the room so that it divided the space into two sections, one an area for dining where the table and chairs sat, and the other an area that comprised a living room, looking out on the deck and the canal. Working it around the end of the couch, Johntie grasped the jacket collar and neatly reversed the body's alignment, beginning to inch it toward the sliding glass panels. Mercer tried to think what they should do once they got it outside, but she shared Johntie's impulse—get it away, out, out of sight. How could they breathe the air in the house until it was cleared of this object that had never belonged there in the first place? And yet, if given the chance to save his life, to pull him in from a rough sea, to administer first aid, she would leap to his side. Given another chance, she would not strike, she told herself. And it was then, just before Johntie gave a final tug that flipped the body around the edge of the couch, causing the highly polished black shoes to disappear from view, that the doorbell rang.

Mercer looked at Johntie in panic, but he of course had heard nothing. She had to answer the summons. It might be the police at the door. It might be word of Benjamin. It might even be Benjamin! She had to go to the door to find out. She need not plan any further than that, no matter who was standing there when she opened the door. Nothing of the recent events in the room could be seen from the door. In fact, nothing could be deduced from the entrance hall or even from the dining area—not unless one crossed the whole room, going around the end of the couch.

Johntie looked up questioningly from his task, wondering why she was not helping him. She signalled to him that someone was knocking at the door, and that she was going to answer. She put a finger to her lips to signify secrecy. He looked alarmed. He walked quickly toward the front door, turned and walked back, gazing at the couch. He shook his head. Not safe enough. He motioned to Mercer to take the man's feet and jerked his thumb toward the sliding glass doors. They would move him to the patio. The doorbell rang a second time. They carried the bulky figure through the glass doors and beyond, past the area that was lit by the light spilling out the doors.

The doorbell rang again, before Mercer could get to the door, and the echo of the bell was chiming in her head as she turned the knob. Susan Peale stood on the wide top step.

"Oh, Susan." Mercer sagged against the door frame.

"Have they found Benjamin?"

"No. Not yet. They are still looking, of course, but they sent me home. They're asking house to house now. Most of what can be done must wait for daylight, apparently. Benjamin comes home from school by a different route than the one I thought he used. As soon as it's light, we'll go over it again and see if I can see anything that might have attracted him, made him stop and look or go in. I'm just . . . staying by the telephone right now."

"I feel so bad. Do you want me to sit with you for a while?"

"No. No, Susan. Thank you. It isn't necessary, really."

"I brought you some Valium," Susan said, reaching into her pocket. She took out a small plastic container and shook several pills into her palm. "It helps. I've been taking them all week. See how calm I am?"

Mercer thanked her and pocketed the pills. She never left medication around where Benjamin might find it. "I'll take one later," she said, "if I decide to try to sleep."

"I wouldn't mind sitting with you for a while," Susan insisted. "Thomas is on the New Orleans-Houston run for a few days. No one to slave for," she added laconically. Mercer sensed that the woman's intention was stronger than just a neighborly gesture. She was determined to stay. *How can I stop her?* she wondered, as Susan brushed her aside and walked into the apartment.

"Oh, hi, Johntie," Susan called. The boy was known and liked by all the neighbors. Susan was the only one who talked to him loudly, as if volume could compensate for his deafness.

"Johntie is helping me . . ." Mercer began.

"He won't mind if I talk to you for just a minute, will he?" Susan asked conspiratorially, pulling Mercer over to the dining table and settling herself onto a chair. "He can't hear us," she added reasonably, leaving him out of the conversation with brisk bad manners, turning her face away so that Johntie could not read her lips.

"We were just about to—I really ought to—"

"I didn't tell you where I was today, did I?" Susan went on. "You know my routine—I'm usually here all afternoon, but today I had to go somewhere. I had to keep an appointment."

There seemed to be no way to stop Susan. Mercer waited, staring through the glass doors to the pool of light on the patio. From where the two women sat, nothing out of the ordinary could be seen, not even a shadow. Nothing but Johntie, in the chair beside the couch, where the lamp threw a bright light, sitting with his legs crossed, working on a tangled fishing line he had drawn from his pocket. She could see that Susan was upset about something and was not really her usual self. *Listen to Susan*, Mercer said to herself. *It's important to listen to Susan just now.*

"I was out today because I went—to an abortion clinic." Susan stopped abruptly. Now that she had said what she came to say, she seemed to have to make an effort to go on. "Thomas insisted. He has always said that he doesn't want children. And it was—it was so awful. And when I got home, and found out that Benjamin hadn't come in from school, I felt such panic and loss, but I don't know now if it's for you or for myself. I know Benjamin is all right," she added quickly. "I know he will be found. But my baby is—is lost forever."

Mercer's head began to throb. She rested it in her hand, silently cursing the timing of crises in her life. Her parents had divorced when she was an adolescent, just when she needed them most; on her wedding anniversary, her husband had asked for a divorce; and now, with her child missing, her neighbor was discussing the advisability of having children at all. *I really can't do any more than I'm doing now*, she thought. But she asked, "Are you all right, Susan? I mean, do you feel well?"

"Oh, yes, it was nothing. I mean, in that way, physically, it was nothing. But there were these people. Demonstrators. There was a dreadful scene in front of the clinic, and I walked right into it. I didn't know what was going on. To tell you the truth, I was walking like a blind person. The sun was so bright I could hardly see. A group of Right to Lifers were demonstrating in front of the clinic, marching up and down with banners. They were carrying these glass jars—glass laboratory jars— and they were coming right up and shaking them in my face. The clinic is in that building near the mall, with all the steps going up to the front. I was walking up to the door, thinking about I don't know what, and people were chanting and yelling. It was supposed to be fetuses, what they had in the jars. I don't know if they looked like fetuses. They looked like soft blue marbles. It was awful."

I'm tired, so tired, Mercer thought. "If you wanted a child, Susan, you should have gone ahead and had it."

"Really? But Mercer, if nobody else wants me to—"

"It's your decision. Whatever Thomas says now, he may change—he will change, more than once, he'll go back and forth. Ultimately you have only yourself to depend on. You have to make your own choices. But once you say yes, you will never change your mind. You can't. Anymore than you can change the course of labor once contractions start. You get a sense of inevitability, of—fatedness. You don't realize it yet, Susan, but having a child or not having a child is something a woman does entirely on her own. Everybody in your life might make it seem not to be so. But it is truly a private and singular thing."

"But—deciding by myself! I can't do it. I'd be scared to be that alone."

"You were alone today, weren't you? Whatever you do, be prepared to do it alone. It's the only way things are done. You'll see. And you won't be scared." Sitting with Susan, her forearms crossed patiently in front of her, Mercer remembered childbirth, the long slow inexorable descent into labor. She had entered a narrow path where there were no turnings, a world where there were no options, and she had thereafter always recognized when she was living under the rule of necessity. "A man never has anything in his life remotely like it," she continued. "How could he ever understand? I didn't understand, myself, until I went into labor and gave birth."

Susan looked unconvinced. "All by myself," she protested.

Mercer looked across the table and felt her strength running out. "Then say no. Say no, if that's what you want. The only choice you have is yes or no, and once you make it you run out of choices." Mercer looked around the room, exhausted, and was brought up short when she looked at the door to the patio. What right had she to defend life, in the presence of death? "Susan, you must go now. I have something I must take care of. No, there's nothing you can do here, really. I'll just walk you to the front door and see if any of the neighbors are still up, although I think I've talked to all of them by now."

A few minutes later, Mercer tapped Johntie's shoulder and he put his fishing line away, instantly ready. She entered his world of silence, leading him through the glass doors and out to the patio.

The tide was coming in. She could hear the waves lapping into the brackish calm of their canal, and when her eyes grew accustomed to the darkness, she could see light reflecting off the black water. Across the way, the key of overgrown brush and straggly palm lay silent under the moonless sky. In the east, there was a brightness that foretold a late moonrise.

The body was gone.

She could not believe her eyes, but it was true. Johntie's eyes were sharper than hers, and he was crouched, feeling into the bank of shrubbery. Mercer stayed on the patio and looked down the row of houses, one after the other with a patio, a bit of ground, and a dock. She decided to go down to the end, in case the man had gone in that direction.

She walked along the seawall, listening. All was quiet. Along the row, a light came on in an upstairs room. It's Susan's light, she thought. Thomas was flying this weekend. That was why Susan had had her abortion alone.

Why had she been so positive with Susan, she wondered, when she herself was not so sure about things in general? She had not always had such ideas about having children. She had never thought about it at all, until Cormack began to pressure her to have another. "No, no, not yet," she had said. "I've got to get to a point where I know more about what I'm doing. I feel as if I'm just beginning to get a grip on my life, just beginning to know what I can do. And I don't mind putting you first, and putting Benjamin first, but I don't want a long list of people who come first, before me. Let me think about it for a while."

"It might be worth a quarter of a million in trust funds from Grandma Wharton's side of the family," he had pointed out. "Besides, I'm ready to have another child."

So she had tried to think of having another child. She had tried to think of it as an act of faith. To show Cor that she believed in their marriage. But not yet. She was still thinking that through her own efforts she could make the marriage work, and was still watching to see if it failed.

"Not now, not just now. I don't feel secure enough," she confessed to Cor.

"Why, what do you think is going to happen?" he asked.

The way he asked made her answer very carefully. She sensed that if she gave a negative answer, Cor would work it into a script. "It would be so sad to have another child if things are not going to go well with us," she said.

"Oh, nonsense. Nonsense, Mercer. Come on, come on. Of course we're going to live together happily, for another X number of years, fifteen, twenty years, whatever." So it was true, she thought, that he was no longer seeing that girl, the actress, the one whose name she could never remember.

Still Mercer hesitated. It seemed to her that happiness could lead on and on, but that unhappiness, such as she had begun to feel with Cor, was always the end of something.

So she had one child. "One is enough," Grace

told her. "The experience of being a parent doesn't intensify—it just repeats." And when the time came to run, she picked up her one and only child and ran.

Mercer circled the last house in the row. The development ended on a small point of land that had been cleared but not yet put to any use. Some of the householders wanted to set up a badminton court there, others wanted to use it for parking. The area was empty. Beyond, on the open Intercoastal Waterway, so wide here it was like a lake, the stars provided enough illumination for her to see quite clearly. There was no one there.

She had to find that man, that Joe Dan Stephens. Where was Benjamin, had this man known?

She circled the houses, returning along the front of the row, looking between the parked cars and boats and stopping occasionally to listen. Soon she was back where she had started.

Johntie stood in the light watching for her return. He shook his head, and she shook hers. Could the man have simply walked away? She would have said he was in no shape to go very far, and yet there seemed to be no other explanation.

Johntie indicated the seawall going to the left, where it ended in a tangle of mangrove. At the point where the wall abruptly stopped, a path over the rocks continued on around to the weed-covered key across the canal. Could the man have gone in that direction? She nodded her acquiescence to Johntie. "Let's look."

What had they been thinking of, to push the man out the door? She had felt a revulsion for the body, thinking it lifeless. She had felt a deep frenzy to be rid of it, to get it out, away. Now she was prepared to search all night for him. How could he be lost? Had he staggered away, confused by the blow? He could be suffering from a concussion. He could have collapsed again. They might stumble over him.

A disturbance arose in the depths of the brackish swamp. A beating of enormous wings swept through the trees, and the great blue heron gave a night scream. Mercer might have fallen from the seawall, but Johntie, having heard nothing, was steady, so she held on to him. "Go back," he told her, pointing the way.

She turned. This section of seawall was low, only a couple of feet above the water. It was the darkest part of the night, and Mercer noticed that there were no longer any lights showing from the houses along the canal. What light there was came from the east, where the rising moon was already reflecting off the small lapping waves, making patterns.

She climbed onto the higher section of seawall, and then onto her own deck. She turned to give Johntie a hand, looking down into the canal as she did so.

In the middle of the canal, moving in the shadow of a boat at anchor, a dark head bobbed. She flung her hands to her mouth to catch her scream. There was a noise in her ears that proved to be the sound of her knees cracking against the boards of the deck as she fell. Johntie, alarmed, threw himself against the seawall and over the top and grabbed her arms. He shook her. "What? *What*?"

She pointed, and he watched the canal for a moment. Then he dragged her to her feet, pointing to the dark, bobbing, turning object, then to the trees leaning over the canal. He made a round shape with his hands. "Coconut," he said carefully, then repeated it, until he was sure she understood. Shaken, they came close, peering at each other in the dim light that spilled from Mercer's living room, watching the dread fade and the hope return. The man had simply disappeared.

CHAPTER FIFTEEN

After they had locked the double glass doors and passed through the quiet house, after she had walked Johntie down the lane to his little place, where his friends were waiting impatiently for him to join them for the night boat, Mercer called the police station. She was afraid she might have missed a call; one of the detectives might have telephoned while she and Johntie were out on the seawall, looking for the dead man who had gotten up and walked away. That there had been a change of shift did not surprise her—it must be long after midnight. She spoke to a detective who was a stranger to her, but who seemed familiar with her situation.

"We'll be starting another house-to-house on this around seven," he told her. "We won't contact you before nine, nine-thirty, so try to get some rest."

"What do you think has happened to him?" she asked.

"Was the boy worried—unhappy—about anything at home?"

"No."

"There was no reason he'd be reluctant to come

home? He wasn't facing discipline or anything like that?"

"No."

"I think we'll find him, fallen asleep—in somebody's garage, somebody's tree house or pool house. We'll check everything out."

"Thank you," she said, able to picture Benjamin asleep, able to think of him now with less fear than at any other time during the long day.

She turned off all the lights downstairs, leaving the one burning over the front door on the street side of the building. She went upstairs slowly, wondering if she would be able to sleep, or if anxiety would grasp her like a great bird with paralyzing talons as soon as she gave herself over to the waiting bed.

If Cormack had Benjamin again, would she ever be able to get him back? She reached into her pocket and plucked out one Valium, two, as if they were candies, and swallowed them dry.

Instead of the expected anxiety attack, she sank into a fantasy as sleep approached, a sort of Grimm's fairy tale in which Benjamin was being tucked into a trundle bed by an elderly couple, a grandfather and grandmother, so lonely for a little boy that they had stolen one from the school yard, brought him home to a feast of crackers and milk, and cake with pudding over the top, and had tucked him under a patchwork quilt. Tomorrow they would quietly sell their house and leave for some distant, unheard of place—a crossroads in West Texas, a sheep station in Australia—where

Ben would grow up without parents to be the cowboy he had sometimes dreamed of being.

She thought about Benjamin, growing up away from her. She wondered what he would remember about her. What did she remember about her own parents, from just the first six years of her life? Her father's fussy perfectionism, her mother's effortless grace. Those were the years when her father had moved them into one house after another, each bigger than the last, each with a better address. As he decided how and where his family would live, he taught her mother to be rich—and it turned out she could do it even better. She was good at being rich—she was terrific. Once she got the hang of that sort of life, she was really very good at it, and beat him at his own game. He'd say, maybe you'd like to decorate a new house. We'll move. And she'd do it, and she'd do it beautifully. He'd say, maybe you'd like some new clothes, a new wardrobe. And she'd come home with marvelous, chic clothes. He'd teach her a sport, and she'd turn out to be superb at it. He lost her to golf and tennis and the life around the pool, the idle friendships at the country club, long before he lost her to the bottle. But that was later. Mercer could just remember her parents as young, restless, ambitious, forever correcting her manners and speech.

Would Benjamin remember the long afternoons in Central Park, Mercer pushing him on a swing, Mercer a watchful presence behind a book while he engineered marvels in the sandbox? She hoped she had given him a picture of herself, something more than their daily routine of playground, nursery suppers, bath ritual. She remembered that her mother loved the scent of tea roses, had filled her bedroom with the small, fat, dripping blossoms, had matched the scent exactly with a potion of her own mixing. The smell of roses now brought her mother back more intensely than demographic memories of where and how they had lived.

"Nutmeg is my favorite spice," she had recently said to Benjamin while she worked in the kitchen. *But what kind of information is that*, she wondered. *It hardly illuminates my personality.* "I think I am an honorable person," she had informed him, driving somewhere in the car, but she wondered if she really was. She had not been strictly honorable with Cormack. She had lied to him. She had told him she was pregnant, when she was not.

Although it might have been true. It was possible that she could have been pregnant when she told Cormack she was. He had stared at her, white with anger, and said, "No, it's impossible. I haven't—"

"The night of the debate," she replied. She saw that he had forgotten. "Our anniversary," she added. She watched his face change and change again as parts of that night came back to him. Then he glared at her with his familiar angry face. It could be true.

"All right, then," he said. "You keep it. You keep this one, I'll take Benjamin."

Why had she told him she was pregnant? *It wasn't a trap*, she insisted to herself. It was a test. She had wanted to find out if Cormack felt a deep, compulsive tie to a child, a child of his, or if he insisted on having custody of Benjamin because he knew him now, knew what an attractive and satisfying child he was, a feeling anybody who knew Ben might have. And because at the time she was afraid it might be true. She was worried about being discarded, abandoned, thrown away —it was a legal ploy that hadn't brought a single advantage. "You can have it. I'll take Benjamin," Cor said. Her lie did nothing but make things more complicated.

No, it did more than that. It was the alarm over the possible legal complications of another pregnancy that got her back into the Fifth Avenue apartment, back into her own bath and dressing room and books and records, after she returned from Silvermine. It had resulted in Cor being in the country and herself in the city. Cor chose Connecticut and ceded Manhattan to her. When she found that he had mounted his legal attack on her, she had stuck her belly out and tormented him every time they met, in the presence of lawyers and financial advisers. "Perhaps I spoke too soon," he began to say.

"Wait a minute, Cor," one of his advisers said. "This child could challenge the disposition of your grandmother's estate."

She laughed at him, but she stopped laughing when the judge in Connecticut gave everything to Cor. "Cor knows every judge in the state," she told Grace. "I know one judge because Cor told me to play tennis with his wife. Cor has money, power, and lawyers. I have a pocketful of credit cards—Mrs. Benjamin Cormack McCormack III, they say. I have a junior partner in Cormack's law firm to give me an allowance and countersign my checks, and no power at all since the judge explained what happens when someone has been 'treated' for a nervous disorder. Especially when that person has walked right up and signed herself in. If you commit yourself to an institution, then you're neurotic, you can't spring yourself. A catch-22 situation, right?"

After that, Mercer dropped the pose of being pregnant and got ready to run. This time she would be clever. Really clever, she thought, and was still thinking she had been when the sound of Quinn's accelerating car made her throw away *The New York Times* and run until she thought her heart would burst, chasing a speeding car down a dusty Long Island road.

To tell the truth—and the Valium made her quite relaxed about being truthful—she had rather liked being on the run. She had felt she really knew herself when she was alone. She had felt free more than she had felt hunted. She had grown competent; just getting herself and Ben through each day attested to her competence.

But it had ended here, in a coastal fishing village whose faint seediness was its only charm. She lay in her bed, stiff and numb, alone as she had never been alone in her life before. She had no idea what would happen now. She could have killed a man—with as little thought as turning off a radio. She had felt that she had to stop him, that she had a right to stop him. Was that the Mercer who always considered herself as having regard and respect for her fellow man? *I love courtesy*, she thought. *I love rituals that acknowledge and guard the rights of others. I love four-way stops. Isn't a four-way stop the essence of courtesy and good sense? Oh, how could I have done such a thing?*

Down the hall, there was no child sleeping.

She heard him scramble up the supporting wall below the terrace and vault over the iron rail of the balcony. He fumbled at the latch for a moment, then was through the flimsy sliding screen and burrowing into her bed, his curls damp, his arms reaching for her.

Her own arms went around his waist and her fists knuckled into his backbone. He polished her shoulders with his rough, flat palms. She rubbed her face into his neck, where the salt from the sea left a dry shine of crystals. His fingers went searching and scraping along her scalp. Her strokes scoured and kneaded. They were literally grooming each other; she had seen primates at the zoo give each other this kind of attention. She massaged his wrist and picked off a flat, round pearly disc that caught the moonlight drifting through the light gauze curtains. Look at this, she thought. A tiny, perfect fish scale. Round as an eye. Clear as glass, but tough, layered. He is turning into a sea creature.

She took and gave comfort as a creature would, and the activity completely absorbed her. His touch soothed. The bed became a nest, a den, a lair. Warmth radiated from them, then settled over their heads and enveloped them. They put their arms around each other and rubbed and pressed. Their breath on each other's face was softer than words. Their thighs met and ground together, and after all the warmth and the melting together, it cooled her—it cooled her from the center.

She slept dreamlessly, and when she woke, tangled and wrapped in Johntie's sleeping limbs, bits and pieces of the day before began to filter into her mind. She had thought she was letter-perfect at visualizing Benjamin's way home. Now, pulling herself out of sleep, with thoughts and images rushing back in quick recapitulation, she realized that she remembered more. She remembered the day they had looked at the cannon, black, squat. It really worked, the old woman had said. Someday, Benjamin might be allowed to fire it all by himself.

She tapped Johntie firmly on his shoulder to rouse him and leaped out of bed, reaching for her clothes.

She knew where Benjamin must be.

CHAPTER SIXTEEN

Mercer pushed her shopping cart along the fruit and vegetable aisle of Briney Breeze's biggest supermarket. She meant to make all of his favorite dishes for Benjamin tonight—never mind that the menu seemed a bit eccentric—and she lifted a whole watermelon into her basket. It was their first night back to normal, or what had come to seem normal. Her goal now was to have an ordinary day go by in an ordinary, routine manner. This evening she and Benjamin would take their meal out to the table set on the seawall. Maybe the old blue heron would come down to the opposite bank of the canal for his evening stroll. Then, afterward, there would be homework and perhaps a little television. It was possible, Mercer found, to look forward to that sort of evening with the keenest anticipation.

She picked up two large golden Spanish onions. Benjamin loved French onion soup, an odd favorite for a child, but he had been very clear in his demands: Onion soup, spaghetti, and watermelon. *Whatever he wants*, she thought, smiling, *he can certainly have*. She had felt giddy and carefree since she got him back. It was a state of euphoria that Benjamin called "stamp happy." This was his name for the gleeful and satisfied feeling he got when he pasted a coveted stamp in his album. She was stamp happy, all right. Her life was all in place once more. She was sure she would never lose Benjamin again. No, that was not quite right—she was sure he would never be lost to her and to himself as well. She was not so possessive as to think he would not leave her for all sorts of reasons—school, friends, lovers. It would happen many times. He might even choose—when he was older, when the choice was his to make—to live with Cormack. She faced the fact that it would be a tempting life. Sailing in Connecticut in the summer, the diversions of the city in the fall. Mercer hoped he would not be faced with making the choice. Or at least not until his defenses were impregnable. Choices and changes would come, she was sure. But the sort of freakish incident that had just taken place—Benjamin spirited away by a total stranger—could not possibly happen again.

Not that she was ever entirely free of anxiety. As long as she was at work and Benjamin was at school, she held it at bay. It was when she left the office that a tic of apprehension began. She always felt she was leaning forward, off balance, in her rush to get home. Her breathing became shallow, and she even found herself holding her breath for long moments. It had been a capricious event, she would remind herself, a lonely woman, a friendly child. Not a repeatable situation.

Mercer had been with the squad car that found

Benjamin. Two houses away from the Revolutionary War cannon reproductions that guarded the gates of Century Acres, the old woman who came to the door admitted that she had "a little visitor."

"This is a nice, clean house," she said proudly to Mercer and the two detectives, "just right for a nice little boy who promises not to run his bike over the lawn. And I gave him bread and milk, with cinnamon and sugar over it. He ate it all up!"

They pushed their way in, responding to the woman with soothing empty talk but moving with determination through all the rooms of the house. Benjamin was asleep, in a locked bedroom.

Mercer's hands went over him rapidly, checking every small limb, as she gazed into his sleepy eyes. His shoes were missing and his T-shirt was grimy, but otherwise he was just as she had last seen him.

"She told me it was okay for me to fire the cannon, Mom," he explained in a whisper. His fingers and arms, his nose and forehead, were cold—as they always were when he was scared or excited. Mercer rubbed his fingers between hers. She remembered once, such a long time ago, when she and Cormack took Benjamin to the circus for the first time. He turned blue with cold. They had wrapped him in their coats, and from deep inside the woolen nest he had peered out at the clowns and elephants. Now his teeth chattered as he looked up from the bed at Mercer. "We went to the lady's house to get the carbide for the charge. I would have been so careful, Mommy! But she locked the door." He was silent for a moment. "Why did she?"

"She is old and a little confused, darling. And probably very lonely. We don't know exactly why she did it. I'm so glad we found you. I don't know why I didn't think of looking around here sooner. I was thinking of other possibilities, I guess. But I had forgotten this funny old lady. I had forgotten that she told you you could shoot off the cannon. Come on, sweetie. Let's find your shoes and go home."

Mercer got down on her knees and looked under the bed. "Hey, here are your sneakers!" she said. She knelt by the side of the bed and put her arms around the little boy. "Can you put them on by yourself? I'll be right back. I'm just going to the next room for a minute."

Now there were three police officers in the living room of the bungalow. One was on the phone and another was working on his notes. The third was a policewoman, who was talking quietly to the old woman.

"My little boy's all right, you know," Mercer said. "What are you going to do with her?"

"We're taking her over to the Bethesda Hospital first. Get her mental and physical condition checked out. We've located her doctor."

"She is really very old, isn't she? Does she have anybody? Anyone you can notify? Is there a neighbor who will go with her?"

"Listen, ma'am," said one of the men. "We'll take it from here. You just see about your little boy."

* * *

That night, Mercer talked to Benjamin when they were home again, just the two of them. "I know, I know," she said, "we talked about shooting off the cannons. But we didn't really know her, baby." She saw that Benjamin didn't see her point.

"Next time," she lectured him, "next time when you do something that's not on the schedule—not the regular thing we do every day—ask yourself, will Mommy know where I am? Will she figure it out? Because if I don't know anything about it, you'll have to wait and check it out with me."

"But, Mommy, you did know. You found me. Didn't you?"

She sighed. "I really liked it better when you were younger and asked me only questions that I could answer. Look at it like this, Ben. Throughout your whole day, you are on a path. Your path leads you to certain places—school, library, art class, all the regular places. And you're sort of on a time schedule too. So at a certain time, you are at a certain place . . . and then, at the right time, you wind up right at your own doorstep. Now, whenever you get off your path, when you go and do something that's not on the schedule, or you spend too much time at one place, so that you are not where you're supposed to be next—then we've got a problem." She wondered if she sounded too much like her father. "I know it's hard, but it's the only way. When you're at school, you don't have to worry about me or wonder where I am.

When I'm at the office, I need to know where you are, or I will get terribly worried."

"I know, Mom. I didn't mean to worry you."

"That's okay now." She wrapped her arms around him and rocked him a little, back and forth. "Now ask me an easy question," she invited, to see if there was any further anxiety about the past forty-eight hours. Benjamin reached for a stack of comic books behind his night table.

"How long can I stay up, Mom?" he asked.

"As long as your candle lasts," she replied. It was an old ritual. Benjamin could read his comics until his eyelids drooped and he fell asleep.

Mercer pushed her shopping cart around a corner, into the aisle where mounds of plastic-wrapped cuts of meat were displayed. Where did they keep the Italian sausage? she wondered. Walking along, glancing from side to side, she spied a curiously familiar shape moving along the aisle in front of her. There was something about the wide haunches, the longish slicked-down fair hair . . . She pushed her cart faster, until it was almost pulling her along. Then she ran it into the man full force, catching his ankle and bringing him up short.

"Owww!" The man howled in indignation and turned on her, but Mercer held him off with the cart.

"You're not dead!" she exclaimed. "Why didn't you let me know?"

"Yeah, I'm alive and walking around—no thanks to you," Joe Dan Stephens said in an aggrieved tone, rubbing his ankle. "You know, I ought to report you. I ought to *sue* you." He paused, as if to give her a chance to apologize. But she felt no guilt, only indignation.

"You made a great deal of trouble for me," she said, "at a time when I already had more than I could manage. My little boy was lost, coming home from school, and at first I thought you had something to do with that. You behaved so mysteriously, and you wouldn't explain yourself. I'm truly relieved that you're not dead, but you did deserve what you got. I'm not sorry. Now I want to know what it was all about."

He put both his hands up in the air, as if fending her off. "Let's just forget about it," he said, as if he were doing her a favor. "I'm a reasonable man. I should be on your case; I've got every right to complain. I could have caught pneumonia. I could have drowned!" He warmed to his complaint. "You're lucky, lady, that I'm willing to drop it."

"But I'm not willing to drop it. What is this all about? Why did you come to my house?"

Stephens looked at her in exasperation. "I'm security," he blustered.

"What?"

"I work in security. For the old man."

"For—you work for the newspaper?" She stammered over her words. It was an answer she had never thought of. "You work for the publisher?"

"Too right I do." He reached into the inside pocket of his cotton jacket and flashed a badge, somewhat shyly. "Security," he pronounced again. "The old man keeps files on everybody. Didn't you know that? There ain't anything about you he can't find out. I know what numbers are on your long-distance telephone bills. I know what letters are sitting in your mailbox. Only I couldn't pick up much on you. No credit rating. No previous address. No record of traffic offenses. No previous employment record. Well, it looks kind of funny, don't it?" He gave a weak smile. "Maybe you've got your reasons. Maybe they don't have anything to do with the paper or the old man." He winked. "Why don't you tell me a little bit about it?"

She understood now who this man was. She understood and relaxed, without losing her anger.

"My life is none of your business. I have a job to do, and I do it. But my private life belongs to me. If I see you again, you'll be sorry. And you can tell the old man that for me. Now, get out of my way or I'll run you down." She brandished her cart at him threateningly.

When she pushed past him, she forgot the list in her pocket and headed for the checkout counter. She felt righteous anger, yet at the same time she felt a certain relief. There were no more loose ends. Life was going to be normal again. The fish jumping in the canal, the dead raccoon on the road, the crazy questions coming across her desk, the weight of the sun, were all part of a normal life that she could fit into, even relish. Benjamin was at home. Stephens had not been sent by Cormack, and her life was back on the rails. Now that she knew she did not have to run again, she felt almost sentimental about the slightly seedy sleepy fishing village where she lived on a canal at the end of a dusty road.

She loaded the groceries into her car and realized she had bought too much. She had felt too expansive, too hungry. She had bought delicacies, lamb chops and smoked fish and spiced cheese, as if she were still setting her table on Fifth Avenue. She and Benjamin had become accustomed to peanut butter sandwiches and tuna casserole. Now she'd nearly blown her week's budget on expensive fare.

She transferred the brown paper bags and the watermelon to the car, and pushed the shopping cart back to its stand. Benjamin had come through so bravely, she was thinking. She wondered where his staunchness came from. He had never been exhorted to bravery, as she had been as a child. She had been pushed to do things she was afraid of, as if such experiences would automatically make her courageous. Whenever she showed any kind of timidity, it became a family project to push her into conquering it. Swim hard against the current, don't panic. It was the same with any kind of fear: Be brave in the surf, right your canoe, get back on the horse.

Benjamin cried when he was hurt, quickly and quietly. He cried from anger, sometimes, when rage or frustration were too great for his small frame to bear. And sometimes now he cried alone, from missing his home and the way things used to be. She sensed that no matter how well things were going now, no matter how happy he was with school and baseball and fishing and fixing up his bike, the only arrangement he would ever really settle for was the old one—to be a child at home, with Mommy and Daddy just down the hall. Wonderful, the way a lost Eden stays green in the heart.

She drove into the parking spot in front of the town house and honked the horn. "Hey, Ben," she called up toward the kitchen window. "Come and help with the groceries." She got out of the car and picked up one bag, fumbling with her keys. There were two locks on the front door, and they always used both.

The hallway was dim, but the light was on in the kitchen. "There's another bag in the car," she called, looking around the kitchen door into the el of the kitchen.

Benjamin stood on a chair beside the kitchen cabinets, beaming at her. He was holding the receiver of the wall telephone, which was higher than he could reach without dragging in a chair from the dining table. He carefully hung up the receiver. "Hi, Mom, guess what? Daddy can come to my birthday. He can come!"

Mercer sagged against the frame of the door, still cradling the bag of groceries, and stared at him. There was really nothing she could say to that happy face. But she managed, "How nice," rapidly calculating how fast she could pack, how soon they could leave, how much money she had on hand—after buying groceries, almost nothing, she realized—whether the car needed gas and oil.

And where would they go this time?

"Was he at home, sweetie? When you called him, I mean. Can you remember what number you dialed? Was he in the city or in Connecticut?"

Benjamin slid down off the chair. He was picking up alarm from her questions. He looked confused. "I don't know," he said, and resolutely stuck to his answer.

"I didn't even know you knew how to dial New York," she said. "I didn't think you would remember the old phone number. I guess I just forget how big you're getting to be. Can you bring in the other bag of groceries from the car? I'll get the melon—it's enormous."

Benjamin bolted for the door in relief, and Mercer rubbed her face with her hands. It was too late to cash a check tonight. But she could pack tonight, and decide what to do. She could go into the office the next morning and pick up her paycheck. She could go to the office early, in fact, and the bank opened at 8:30—the drive-in windows did, anyway. She and Ben could be on their way by nine o'clock.

On their way where?

Well, they could go west this time. That would be a change. They could cross the state below Lake Okeechobee, drive through the Panhandle, and go west.

She found herself thinking of west as a location, not a direction. But at what point would they find a place to stop? She sighed, thinking, *Quinn, your job is not as difficult as I once thought. People do reach a point when they want to give up, to be found.* Perhaps it was time she dropped out. Perhaps she had run her own life as long as she was going to be allowed to.

Her mother had believed that part of being wise was knowing when to give up, and she had done so fairly early. Her father, on the other hand, would call such an attitude defeatist. He had raised Mercer to be a winner. As he had been. She remembered—although she had been very young—the time when he began to be successful, to make it in the consulting field. *And then we began to be rich*, she remembered. *We all learned quickly. Lesson piled on lesson.*

What would Daddy say if he could see me now? she wondered. *On the run in a secondhand Plymouth. Watching old Charles Bronson movies until I believed that I could stop the violence in my life with violence. . . .*

Benjamin came in with the groceries, and she let him unpack all the expensive, special foods she had spent her last bit of cash on.

Mercer spent the next hour packing and filling the car with those things she had decided would continue to be necessary. The backseat could hold nothing more. And yet the number of things she was leaving behind was considerable. Funny, she thought, every time she moved on, she chose differently. This time, for example, she was ready to jettison the Queen Anne candlestick.

What time was it? Eight-thirty. The time was passing. Benjamin had made his call around six.

"I have an idea," she said to him when they were finishing their meal. "Let's check in to a motel for the night. One with a swimming pool. Then we can have a nice swim and go to sleep all cool and relaxed. It will be like a little vacation. Want to?''

"No," said Benjamin.

It took a while to talk him into it, but finally the two of them locked the house and drove to one of the many tourist places on U.S. 1, picking one that boasted a slide going into the pool. Benjamin began to think it was a good idea after all. Later, waterlogged, he slept deeply as Mercer watched the TV screen with blank eyes and waited for the morning.

She left the motel as early as she could the next morning, leaving Benjamin, still asleep, in the care of the retired couple who ran the place. She hoped to get to the office by the time the first employees arrived in the payroll department. She'd have to wait while they calculated her paycheck, then dash over to the bank to draw the money.

She seemed to be moving slowly, despite her timetable and many cups of hot coffee. She recognized a certain dragging reluctance in herself, an unwillingness to keep moving. And yet moving on seemed to be the only means she had of retaining independence, of staying in control. Like the outlaws in the old movies. The plot was this: An outsider became an outlaw through a longing for independence. He might be driven to abandon his path by the pressures around him—by impositions, compulsions, disorder, injustice. It became harder to maintain independence, until existence itself became a brutalized form of independence.

Then he might feel that the cost of independence was too high. That must be the meaning, the message, in the lines of resignation stamped on Charles Bronson's face. How many times, she wondered, had she seen Clint Eastwood's flesh scraped and bloody? Clarity to the bone is the result. Every choice becomes a blow. And somewhere ahead is the moment when violence is a weapon in your hand, and the desire to grasp it is more seductive than love.

CHAPTER SEVENTEEN

Mercer headed for the interstate highway for the fast run into town. There was very little traffic; too early yet for the morning rush. There was no one at all in the northbound lane ahead of her as she sped up the ramp, and only one vehicle moving up behind.

The morning was already warm, the sun a white ball hanging over the ocean. The car behind overtook her and moved into the center lane, preparing to pass her on the right. She was annoyed at the driver's carelessness. He had almost brushed her rear right wheel. The idiot. The whole road to himself and he couldn't keep his distance.

As she said to Quinn later, "It was so peaceful. Almost no traffic. Do you know how it happens sometimes when you are driving along and another car slowly overtakes you, and for a brief period you are moving along exactly parallel to each other? If you're traveling at the same speed, you lose any sense of movement, because there's no contrast—you both seem to float, suspended over the roadbed.

"If you glance over just at that moment, you see the other driver, only a few feet away. You get this funny—almost social—feeling, as if you're two people seated comfortably in the lobby of the Algonquin, waiting for the waiter to bring your drink.

"Well, I was driving to the office with a lot on my mind, and I looked over at the car in the lane next to me, and there was Cormack, slightly reclining in his seat, gazing straight ahead. And he looked the way he always looks. He looked the way he looks sitting at his desk. Just the same. He didn't even glance over at me. But his car came a little closer, almost into my lane. There was practically no traffic going north, a little more going south, toward Fort Lauderdale.

"And all of a sudden I felt all right about whatever was going to happen. Maybe it was a rush of adrenaline, I don't know. Because Cormack had been unfair to me before, or unfeeling, or even mean; but he had never sort of declared himself outside where we still negotiated from a common ground of some kind. But I knew now that he was going too far. Clarity. It was the first time I understood how you could be released from the obligation to behave well. I guess it doesn't happen until . . . well, until you've been pushed to that point. I don't know now where that point is exactly. I don't know if I will ever be there again. In the kind of lurid way I was thinking then, it was as if I were wearing a black leather jacket, and had just zipped it up to my chin."

The car in the center lane edged closer again. Mercer held her course. There was the faintest whisper of contact, not enough to rock the car but enough to sound in her ears.

She was totally on guard. "Do you know how to run this thing?" Someone had asked Charles Bronson that ridiculous question. "I think so," she said out loud. It was Bronson's line. She tried to say it with the same certainty.

For the first time, Cormack glanced across the narrow chasm that divided them. His eyes widened for a moment as they stared at each other.

"Get out of my way!" she shouted at him through the open window of the car, and the wind took her words and spun them away. It was the first time, she told Grace later, that Cormack had ever looked at her as if he had lost count. Had she fired six bullets? Or was it only five?

Cormack looked straight ahead. He probably thought he was panicking her, she realized. A year ago it might have worked.

Where were they? She checked the road. They were passing Exit 44, and were about a minute short of the exit she took to reach the office. The next exit was coming up quickly. The exit ramp, on the right, dropped sharply, but the highway itself lifted some sixty feet above the east-west road that bisected it below.

Mercer felt the adrenaline rush as it pushed her system into high gear; her carbohydrate metabolism speeded up, increasing her supply of quick energy; her blood vessels readied themselves, became narrowed and pinched by the release of nor-adrenaline, the body's way of reducing the danger of hemorrhage. The quick supply of blood to heart, lungs, and brain made her feel momentarily as light and clearheaded as she had ever felt in her life.

She took a deep breath.

Mercer hooked to the right, slightly, quickly, meeting Cormack's slow, threatening drift. She was ready for the impact and adjusted for it instantly, slamming on her brakes and steering for the center verge to her left, sliding and throwing up clumps of dirt and saw grass behind her.

Cormack's car was thrown to the right by the impact. Before he could bring it back toward the center of the road, it was airborne. Mercer, in one sideward glance, saw it leave the road and fly for an instant before it dropped out of sight.

Her car was moving faster than she intended, even though she had been standing on the brakes since the moment she brushed against Cor's fender. She was prepared to come up hard against the concrete wall that protected the central shaft in the overpass against the drop to the highway underneath, even to crash against that wall, but the impact came with devastating force. The front of the car crumpled and she was flung into the dashboard. Her forehead snapped against the windshield, but more critically her neck was driven against the steering wheel. Something was jamming into her head from the rear, and she could not free herself. Her windpipe was crushed against the steering wheel. She could not breathe. Her mouth filled with the warm taste of iron. The deep breath she had taken seconds before still fed oxygen to her brain. With it, she had given herself another thirty seconds of consciousness.

She could not seem to shift the weight from the back of her shoulders. Her flailing, clenching hand groped along the dashboard; some dim memory told her there was an object there, a tool, something . . . Her fingers identified it before her mind labeled it with a name.

Crushed and suffocating, with the brightness of the morning hanging like a curtain over the wrecked car, Mercer performed a makeshift tracheotomy on her own flesh with the pointed hollow of the broken ballpoint pen that had been rattling around on the dashboard since the first day of school. It gave her another three minutes of life, pinned between the seat of the car, wedged in place by an upended suitcase in the backseat, and the twisted steering wheel. The three minutes were enough time for a passing motorist in the northbound lane and a truck driver in the southbound lane to reach the ruined car and together drag the limp, bleeding form from behind the wheel.

CHAPTER EIGHTEEN

Mercer heard a familiar voice, but faintly, as if from a great distance.

"So he was a villain, after all," said the voice.

She tried to open her eyes, but she could not make it happen. She felt fragmented—alive in some parts, vastly separated from other parts that still slept. Something located in her chest seemed raspingly awake, but her eyelids could not be forced to move.

Quinn was there when she opened her eyes. The first thing she saw was the light gleaming off his James Joyce eyeglasses. She tried to speak, but all her efforts produced only a faint whisper.

"Quinn! How did you know . . . how did you know where to find me?"

He put his finger to his mouth. "Don't try to talk now. Plenty of time later. They tell me you're going to be all right."

"But how did you know?"

"They called me."

"They . . .?"

"Found my business card in your wallet. Idiot,"

he added softly, "didn't I train you better than that?"

She stopped trying to talk and began to look around. In her field of vision she could see a hospital bed, a white cotton gown, a pillow. She touched the gauze and tape at her throat.

"Leave it alone, now, or I'll call the nurse," Quinn threatened, taking her hand away.

"Ben?" she asked.

"He's fine. He's over at your neighbor Susan's, minding the dogs. He's very good with dogs. Should have one of his own, perhaps."

She tried to nod, but her head was too heavy to move. She felt herself drifting off again. If she could just sleep another hour or two, she thought, then she'd wake and be able to cope. What else should she ask Quinn? Wasn't there something else?

"Cor?" she asked.

"He didn't make it," Quinn said bluntly. "The crash was quite terrible, it was all over in a second. I saw the place myself." He sat silent for a while.

"As we've pieced it together," he went on in his private investigator's voice, "Mr. McCormack was on his way to join you for the boy's birthday. By the greatest coincidence, the two of you happened to be traveling on the road at the same time. As it happens, the highway patrol thinks he was trying to catch your attention and lost control of his car, sideswiped yours, and shot off the overpass. At least that's how it appears to them." He watched her. "There was nothing I could add to their information. I could only be making my own private guesses why he had followed you here and how he happened to be on the road at that hour."

"I meant it to happen," she whispered. What she wanted to explain to Quinn was that she had not acted simply on instinct, an unthinking response, when she maneuvered her car to meet Cor's. But it had not been purely an act of will either. *When I was ready for it to happen*, she thought, *it happened*.

Mercer closed her eyes.

Quinn's quiet, dry voice continued. "It is not easy," he said, "to know the man's motives. He followed his own will. Thank God I was not an instrument of it this time. I would not want to aid a man to such an end."

She opened her eyes again and comforted herself with the sight of Quinn. Making no concessions to climate, he sat there in his tweed suit, his eyes full of concern for her. *You are the most . . . equable man*, she thought, but was not able to say it. Her eyes seemed to close more than once, closing on themselves again and again.

Mercer is sitting on the beach. She faces the sea, her legs drawn up, her arms wrapped around her knees. Her back is bare, and the sun burns across her shoulders. Around her neck she wears a jingle shell that Johntie has found and threaded on a piece of blue yarn. It hides the small round scar of the self-inflicted tracheotomy that saved her life. Benjamin is riding the waves, and she looks up from time to time to see if he is all right. He has just learned to bodysurf, and he throws himself forward again and again onto the crest of a wave.

Mercer has not yet moved away from the narrow town house on the canal. She is still in the small, white-baked Southern town. Perhaps she is waiting for the school year to end. Perhaps she is waiting until she feels stronger.

She is trying to deal, with a certain amount of horror, with the idea that she now has everything that once belonged to Cor. It is a side effect of what happened on the highway. On the highway she had wanted to win, yes, but now she can hardly deal with winning. She has Cor's name again . . . still. She is executor of his estate, because she is Benjamin's parent and guardian. The money, the bulk of the family fortune, it turns out, is all for Benjamin. This is not Cor's doing, but Cor's grandmother's doing, a woman Mercer had never known, but whose warm flannel gowns she has frolicked in. The family, it seems, has lived on whatever individual capital or trust funds each had come into. No one in Cormack's family has added substantially to the family money in three generations. All in a holding pattern, waiting for the main portion of the estate to pass down. Now she found that the family fortune— the bulk of the estate that was gathered in one place and could be called a fortune—had been left by the old woman to the one great-grandchild born to her before her death, whom she had never seen but whose name had reached her in the clinic in Switzerland. She had drawn up a will that was limiting and absolute. No further issue could benefit.

Now Mercer could date the moment when Cor stopped urging her to have another child. It was after the reading of his grandmother's will. That was why, when she tried to play her phony trump card, he had said, "You keep that one. I'll take Benjamin."

These matters are of a size and complexity that she cannot begin to think about yet. She has Benjamin. She has a flaming death to remember. She has a scar that imprints itself on her fingertips every time her hand unthinkingly lifts to touch her throat. She feels in some way permanently damaged, yet in another way permanently mended. She will go back after she has thought about things for a while. Quinn has gone back already, to manage things for her until she can pack her belongings and return to New York. Oh, yes, she will take her baggage with her: The framed photographs, the Queen Anne candlestick, Ben's toys, her books. That little pile of belongings that had more than once defined her needs.

She picks up a sliver of driftwood, a splinter from some mast or hatch. She digs in the sand. She would like, she realizes, to actually bury Cor, to literally bury Cor. To dig his grave, to labor in the earth, to put his body away, to fill in the hole and cover the grave over, to smooth out the earth with her hands. More than anything, she wants to bury him, bury Cor in the sand and in the past, cover him up with time and earth and forgetting.

Someday, she thinks, *the time will come when I will not even remember Cor any longer. Not the way he looked or the sound of his voice or the ways in which I tried to please him. I will not remember what he wanted or how he tried to get it. If I live for a very long time, then I will have known Cor for only a very small portion of my life. And for part of that time, I really hardly knew him or myself because I was always thinking of him as a husband, a businessman, a father, and of myself as someone fitting into his life and making it work. We were gazing at two images in a mirror, not looking at each other at all.*

What I still don't know, she thinks, *is how far anyone is allowed to go to get what he wants. Cor set no limits on what he would do to get what he wanted. I don't believe that can be right, but I don't know what my grounds are for saying that. Just that it wouldn't work for me. I don't know where the limits are. I can sometimes figure them out from moment to moment. But when it comes down to life or death, it seems as if the decision has been made long ago. I didn't even stop to think, did I? My hand jerked the wheel over. When Cor started his car toward mine, I met him halfway. I will never forget the sound when the sides of the cars came together.*

She pushes the stick through the sand, over Cor's make-believe grave, drawing lines, arcs, paths.

Look, she thinks, *I'm making a garden. That's something I'd like to try to do. An orchard. Pear trees, apple trees, quince. Perhaps we'll keep bees too. The land in Connecticut could be put to use.* She feels ambitious. *Well, I'd like to do this,* she thinks. *I'd like to make things grow.*

She feels unable to do much planning at the moment, but she feels that whatever thinking she is doing now is clear and not confused.

I think I will make a garden, she decides. *I think I will learn all I can about making gardens. I'll go to England and Italy and France. I'll make gardens. I'll make wonderful gardens that people will long to be inside.*

Mercer remembers the house her parents lived in when she was born. It had had a wonderful garden. Her parents had made it, working together in the youth of their marriage. Beyond that garden stretched fields that were full of wildflowers. *We would have been happy,* she realizes suddenly, *if we had stayed there. If we had never left that house and that garden, we would have been a happy family.*

She hears Benjamin as he yells in glee. "Ma, watch!" It brings her back to the present. She lets go of the memory of the garden of her childhood. *No,* she thinks, *we could not have stayed there. The things that happened led me here, to this present moment. I can't imagine any other.*

She sits erect and watches Benjamin cavort in the waves. She has a sense of being centered, of possessing a point of view, of living in the present. It feels like eternity, and it happens exactly at the moment when Ben yells, "Mer-CER! Wheeee!" and she looks up as a wave lifts him and sees her child suspended pale and gleaming and laughing in the wave's green center.

What does she want really? To bear the weight of life, she supposes, and the weight of love, until, like Ina with her young lover, one or the other breaks her bones.

THE LATEST IN BOOKS AND AUDIO CASSETTES

Paperbacks

☐	27032	**FIRST BORN** Doris Mortman	$4.95
☐	27283	**BRAZEN VIRTUE** Nora Roberts	$3.95
☐	25891	**THE TWO MRS. GRENVILLES** Dominick Dunne	$4.95
☐	27891	**PEOPLE LIKE US** Dominick Dunne	$4.95
☐	27260	**WILD SWAN** Celeste De Blasis	$4.95
☐	25692	**SWAN'S CHANCE** Celeste De Blasis	$4.50
☐	26543	**ACT OF WILL** Barbara Taylor Bradford	$5.95
☐	27790	**A WOMAN OF SUBSTANCE** Barbara Taylor Bradford	$5.95

Audio

☐ **THE SHELL SEEKERS** by Rosamunde Pilcher
Performance by Lynn Redgrave
180 Mins. Double Cassette   48183-9 $14.95

☐ **THE NAKED HEART** by Jacqueline Briskin
Performance by Stockard Channing
180 Mins. Double Cassette   45169-3 $14.95

☐ **COLD SASSY TREE** by Olive Ann Burns
Performance by Richard Thomas
180 Mins. Double Cassette   45166-9 $14.95

☐ **PEOPLE LIKE US** by Dominick Dunne
Performance by Len Cariou
180 Mins. Double Cassette   45164-2 $14.95

Special Offer
Buy a Bantam Book
for only 50¢.

Now you can have Bantam's catalog filled with hundreds of titles plus take advantage of our unique and exciting bonus book offer. A special offer which gives you the opportunity to purchase a Bantam book for only 50¢. Here's how!

By ordering any five books at the regular price per order, you can also choose any other single book listed (up to a $5.95 value) for just 50¢. Some restrictions do apply, but for further details why not send for Bantam's catalog of titles today!

Just send us your name and address and we will send you a catalog!